JACK SWORD

AND

THE SEVEN KEYS

The Story of Jack Sword's

adventurous journey to find The Seven Keys to save

the Kingdom from a dangerous Dragon!

Author: Dion George

Year and Month of Publishing: December 2021

Cover Design : Sijo Jordi Perumpillil

Cover Image credit to : kevron2001 (istockphoto.com)

Author

Dion George

Dion George is the author behind the novel **Jack Sword and the Seven Keys**. Dion is 12 years old and lives in Ireland with his family. He is very passionate about his writing and published his first book in 2020, named **Ten Amazing Animal Stories.**

Contents

Chapter 1

The Legend of Rexus

A long, long time ago, a horrible and evil dragon came to the magnificent kingdom of Julandia, and enslaved all of its people. Life was hard for the people of Julandia, as the dragon was so mean and ruthless! People began to call the dragon "Rexus", because it was so mean! The people hated being ruled by the dragon, so seven brave knights decided to stand up to the dragon, and bravely fight it!

The seven knights fought the dragon as hard as they could, and they won! The seven knights locked the dragon up in a massive, strong cage on a volcano, called Irupt Volcano with seven wonderful keys, one for each knight! These keys were magical, because if all seven were locked they transported the dragon into the cage, and if they were all unlocked, they teleported the dragon out of the cage! The kingdom was safe again!

Three hundred years later, the dragon was still alive, and still stuck in the cage, and the Seven Keys were kept safe in the royal castle! But there was one problem... There was a group of people that wanted to use the Seven Keys to free and use the dragon to defeat the king, King Leo, and rule Julandia!

Those people were called "Team Rexfire" they and their boss, Aria had a plan to steal the Seven Keys and use them to unlock Rexus's cage! That's exactly what they did. Some of Team Rexfire snuck into the castle that night and stole the Seven Keys! "Give me the keys!" Aria said, pushily. Aria took the Seven Keys, which were kept in a bright blue leather box, and escaped from the castle, and headed for the cage on Irupt Volcano! Luckily, one of the guards on night duty spotted the group heading out of the castle, and immediately woke up and alerted the king! "King Leo, I believe someone has stolen the Seven Keys!" warned the guard, "Quickly! Go to the volcano!" the King shouted, looking quite tired. The guards quickly ran to the volcano, and when they arrived, they saw a hooded black figure at the top of the volcano, right next to Rexus's cage!

The guards were so shocked that a precious artefact could be stolen so easily! The guards tried to climb up the volcano, but the treacherous terrain meant that it was very hard to climb! Meanwhile, the hooded figure (who was Aria) unlocked the cage, and an evil grin came onto her face! The keys unlocked each lock one by one, and then "Roar!" Rexus came flying out of the cage! The guards fainted when they saw this, and the king spotted it from a distance, and quickly began to write down a letter for the whole kingdom! Meanwhile, Rexus accepted Aria as its master, because she freed it after three hundred years! Aria hopped onto Rexus's back, and holding the Seven Keys, flew away! As they flew, Aria dropped each of the keys all around the kingdom, hoping no one would find any of them.

Now it's time to finally introduce the hero of this story, Jack Sword. Jack Sword was a naive, brave young fellow, who lived in a village called Lighton Village, a quiet farming town. Jack was the son of a farmer, Mr. Sword, but he didn't like farm work at all! Sadly, his mother died when he was very young. Jack didn't like farming, but there was one thing he loved, sword fighting! He practised with his father whenever his father got free time, and he wished he could go on some kind of adventure, and come back as a hero, and make his father proud!

He got the chance to do that, when one fine day, a letter came, addressed from the king, not just to Jack, but to everyone in the kingdom!

Jack opened up the letter, here's what it said:

To,

The Whole of Julandia,

Greetings everyone, I hope you are well. As you may know, Rexus has escaped from its cage on Irupt Volcano, and the Seven Keys have been stolen and scattered across the kingdom. Do not panic about this! I have sent this letter to ask if anyone would like to volunteer to journey around the kingdom, to find all the Seven Keys, and give them all back to me, so we can lock up Rexus again! If you want to volunteer, come to the castle in New Deyal at any time before the 20th of March. You must volunteer quickly, because Team Rexfire could use Rexus to attack me at any moment!

From,

King Leo the Third.

Jack was very excited, this was his chance for an adventure! He brought the letter to his father immediately! But his father did not agree, "No, I don't want to lose you just like you lost your mother!" said Mr. Sword, "But dad, I know sword fighting! I won't be in any danger!" replied Jack, "No, I won't let you!" replied Mr. Sword. Jack was quite a stubborn and determined boy, so he continued to ask, and ask, and ask again! But his father wanted to keep him safe, so he wouldn't agree.

"I need to volunteer before the 20th of March, and it's already the 17th! It takes 1 day to walk from Lighton Village to the capital city, New Deyal, so I need to convince my father to let me go to volunteer tomorrow!" thought Jack, and then he had an idea, "What If I challenge my father to a sword fighting duel, if I win, I can go to find the Seven Keys, If he wins, I stay at home!"

The next morning, Jack told his father his idea, at first he refused, but Jack asked so much that he had to give in. They both took their places inside of a little shed. Mr. Sword was holding a strong metal sword, while Jack was holding a small, wooden training sword. "3, 2, 1," they chanted! The duel began and Jack quickly ran towards his father! The aim of a sword fighting duel was to knock the opponent's sword out of their hand, and Jack tried to do that confidently! Mr. Sword blocked Jack's attack, and as he did not want to hurt his son, he continued to defend himself, but Jack didn't give up, and after several rapid strikes, Mr. Sword lost his grip! Jack Sword had won. "Alright son, you can go to find the Seven Keys, just please be careful, and visit me often, here's my sword, you can have it." said Mr. Sword, "Ok!" said Jack, joyfully, and after packing up his stuff, Jack was ready to begin his adventure. He left the house after saying goodbye to his father, and he was very excited! Jack's quest had begun!

Chapter 2

Glimmer Forest

Jack, who was excited to volunteer to find the Seven Keys, had to journey through the calm, serene Glimmer Forest to get to the capital city, New Deyal, a busy and glamourous city, and the home of the king, King Leo.

Jack walked quickly, because tomorrow was the great day where people would be chosen to go on the quest to find the Seven Keys! Jack admired the beautiful fields, with daisies growing all around, he could even see his father's small farm in the distance! "Goodbye everyone, goodbye Lighton Village!" said Jack as he walked, with his dark brown hair blowing in the wind, and his sky blue eyes watching everything around him! Jack wore a dark navy coat, with shiny black buttons, and dirty grey boots.

Jack arrived at Glimmer Forest about 15 minutes later. "Wow!" he said cheerfully, looking at the Glimmer Berries the forest was named after growing on the trees! "Yummy!" he said as he plucked a Glimmer Berry off of a tree, and he took a big bite of it! "Never had one fresh off of a tree before!" he said, with his mouth full. All of a sudden, Jack heard some rustling in the bushes, and he quickly drew out his sword, in case it was a threat, but then, the unexpected happened! A girl with black hair and green eyes popped out of the bushes! She had a white pet rabbit on her shoulder, and she had lettuce in her pocket.

"Hi there!" she said, "I'm Amy, What's your name?" said the strange girl, "I'm Jack Sword!" replied Jack, "This is my pet, Fluffy! She's really hungry right now, so I was heading to Lighton Village! Would you like to come with me?" asked Amy, "Sure! Make it quick though!" replied Jack, and they walked back to Lighton Village. "Hello, Lighton Village!" they said when they arrived.

"Why did you say we need to be quick?" asked Amy, "I want to volunteer for finding the Seven Keys!" replied Jack, "Cool! I wanted to volunteer too, but I don't know the way to New Deyal!" replied Amy, "Why don't I show you the way?" asked Jack, "Really? Yes! Thank you!" answered Amy, "Squeak!" said Fluffy, when they arrived at the market stalls. "Let's go get some carrots!" said Amy, and she ran to the vegetable stall and bought some carrots for 5 silver coins. Meanwhile, Jack saw Mrs. Rita cross the street, Mrs. Rita was a cranky old lady who always bought milk from Jack's father's farm every day, "Get out of my way!" said Mrs. Rita, "Fine."

said Jack, annoyed. Then, Amy got back from the marketplace, with 3 fresh orange carrots, and gave one to Fluffy, "Munch!" squeaked Fluffy, "Ok! Let's get moving!" said Jack, and they marched back into Glimmer Forest.

Jack ate another Glimmer Berry as they walked, "Isn't this forest beautiful?" said Amy, "Isn't this berry tasty!" said Jack, with his mouth full, again. Suddenly, Fluffy got scared by something and quickly hopped into Amy's bag...

"What is it Fluffy?" said Amy, "Squeak!" squeaked Fluffy, "Oh, no... What is that!" cried Jack, as he drew out his sword, and Amy took out a brown bow, with silver arrows! Suddenly, "Roar!" a strange creature came out of the bushes! It had 3 eyes, 4 legs, and a big mouth with sharp teeth! Amy loaded her bow, but didn't shoot, because it wasn't attacking them, but Jack charged as fast as he could, "Yaaaaah!" he said as he slashed his sword. This made the beast angry, and it charged at Amy! "Shoot Amy, Shoot!" said Jack, but she didn't shoot her bow, instead, she dodged the beast into the bushes, and it looked like she was thinking about something! Jack continued to slash the beast with his father's sword, but it barely made a scratch on the scaly monster! Jack dodged and slashed and dodged and slashed, "This is a good name for a sword technique, Dodge and Slash!" said Jack, as he hit the monster again and again, but then, "What if we feed it berries?" asked Amy, as she hopped out of the bush, "What do you mean?" said Jack, "I think the monster is hungry, and feeding it might calm it down!" said Amy, "Yes! Let's do it!" said Jack.

They both climbed a Glimmer Tree and picked a few Glimmer Berries, Jack ate one of them, but they threw the rest at the beast! The beast charged towards the berries, and while it was eating them, Jack, Amy, and Fluffy ran away as fast as they could.

Meanwhile, at Team Rexfire's secret base, Aria was feeding Rexus to make it strong again, after eating very little for 300 years, it was quite weak. The rest of the team were researching dragons, and they discovered that dragons live for about 500 years! They found out that Rexus was probably 380 years old! Some others were planning the attack on the castle.

Back to Jack and Amy, they had just escaped from the beast! "Hey Amy, when did you get that bow?" asked Jack, "I got it when I was just 7, I'm 12 right now, I really love archery, and I'm pretty good at it too!" replied Amy, "Really! I'm 12 too! Also, why didn't you want to shoot the monster?" said Jack, "I didn't want to shoot the monster because I love animals, even really creepy and scary ones, I knew that it was only attacking you because you hit it!" said Amy, "Ok" said Jack, and Fluffy squeaked again.

They continued to walk through Glimmer Forest and felt calm, and felt the wind on their faces, and light drops of rain began to fall on their heads. The sun was setting, "Let's rest a bit, after all, the volunteering is only happening next afternoon, and my feet are aching from all this walking!" suggested Amy, "Sure!" said Jack, still quite energetic. They both made a campfire, and Jack got his tent out of his backpack, and Amy got hers. They both set up their tents, ate some Glimmer Berries and sandwiches, and went to sleep.

The next morning, they both woke up and continued to walk after a breakfast of, you guessed it, Glimmer Berries (They were getting tired of eating them by now) "Let's go!" said Jack, "I think I see New Deyal in the distance!" They ran until they finally saw a path again, and followed it until they arrived at New Deyal!

"Wow!" said both of them at the same time, they saw golden statues and big building, and fancy, posh, people all around the city! "Let's go explore before the volunteering!" said Jack.

Chapter 3

New Deyal

Jack Sword and Amy Arrow were exploring the capital city of New Deyal before volunteering day at the castle, and they were having fun!

"Let's try food from that restaurant over there Amy!" said Jack, "No thank you, but come here!" said Amy, "What?" asked Jack, "There's a sword fighting tournament, I thought you and your sword could try it!" said Amy, "Of course I want to try it! Come on!" said Jack. They heard one of the judges calling out, "Who wants to challenge the mighty Prince Lucas!" said the judge, and then they saw a young, handsome boy, who was bragging, a lot. "No one can beat me and my golden sword and shield, I can defeat everyone in one hit!" bragged Prince Lucas, "Why is he acting like he's the prince, he's behaving like he's on the top of the world or something!" complained Jack, "He is the prince though! Prince Lucas Shield the First,

I believe." said Amy, "He has a really cool shield, but I don't really like his attitude." said Jack, "He is quite charming though!" said Amy, Suddenly, Jack called out to Prince Lucas, "Hey, Prince Lucas, I challenge YOU to a duel!" Jack screamed.

"Really, this kid thinks he can defeat me!" said Prince Lucas, to the audience, "I'll show you!" said Jack, as he ran down to the stage, "Come at me!" he said. "Really?" said Prince Lucas, surprised at seeing someone who was brave enough to challenge him, "Yes!" said Jack, "Well then, let us battle." said Lucas, "3, 2, 1, Go!"

The two boys charged at each other with great force, both speeding at each other, both of them were very similar in a way, both never giving up, "Dodge and Slash, Dodge and Slash, Dodge and Slash!" said Jack, "Block and Strike!" said Prince Lucas, they continued dashing around the battlefield, but neither of them lost grip of their sword, "Remember, the aim is to knock my sword out of my hand, not that you will though!" said Prince Lucas. "Wow!" said Amy, "Squeak!" said Fluffy, as the boys continued to strike again, and again, neither of them losing concentration, Lucas continually put up his shield again and again!

"You're actually quite decent! What is your name?" said Prince Lucas, "Thanks! My name is Jack, Jack Sword!" said Jack, "Nice, that doesn't mean I'll lose though!" said Prince Lucas, and finally, something crazy happened...

The two swords dropped out of their hands, at the same time! "What!? Unbelievable!" said Prince Lucas, "A draw, against the prince, awesome!" said Jack, but then, they heard the doors bang down... Two Team Rexfire members kicked down the doors to the stadium! "We won't let anyone volunteer today!" said one of them, "What? Oh come on!" said Prince Lucas, "Hey Jack, Do you want to defeat these annoying Team Rexfire maniacs with me?" sighed Prince Lucas, "Of course I do! They're bad guys!" said Jack, "Can I join in too?" said Amy, "She's my friend, Amy!" said Jack, "Sure! Come along then!" said Prince Lucas.

The three of them ran towards the Team Rexfire members and began chasing them away, "Go away, you bad guys!" said Jack, "Yeah, what he said!" said Amy, "Yeah, run away to your little base! Don't come near my father with that dragon of yours!" said Prince Lucas, They all fought and chased away the Team Rexfire members, and by now, it was noon. "It's time for the volunteering ceremony! Let's go!" said Jack, "I need to be there too, so come on!" said Prince Lucas, "Also, you don't have to call me Prince Lucas, just Lucas is fine!"

"Ok!" said Amy, and they ran to the castle, and as soon they arrived at the gateway, someone spoke! "Prince Lucas, are these your new friends?" asked the guard, "Yes!" said Lucas, and they split up when they went inside. The ceremony began, and there were only a few people volunteering! There was a strange old man, a person with a camel and a slingshot, a lady with a really fluffy coat, a few others, and them. Prince Lucas was with his father on a throne. King Leo began to speak.

"Thanks to everyone who decided to volunteer, you are all heroes, I have some information for you all, you are all now officially going to be searching for the Seven Keys, so that we can lock up Rexus again, and defeat team Rexfire. It is a simple but difficult goal, but I know you can do it. Also, whoever collects the most keys also gets a prize of becoming a knight and a lot of money, if you would like. That is all for my speech, I hope you do well on your quests, and I hope you don't get burnt by Rexus, Goodbye." said King Leo.

But then, Lucas went up to his father, King Leo, and asked if he could join Jack and Amy's quest to find the Seven Keys, "Jack is an honourable swordsman, and Amy is a nice archer, so can I join their group?" asked Lucas, "Alright Lucas, I know I can trust you to go alone, so you can go, but please be careful though." replied King Leo, and then he turned to Jack and Amy, after everyone else left, "Jack Sword and Amy Arrow, do you promise to keep my son, Prince Leo Shield the First safe?" asked King Leo, "Yes" replied Jack and Amy. "Ok then, Goodbye to you all!" and the king left with a proud smile! The three of them left the castle, their quest for the Seven Keys had officially begun.

Meanwhile, at Team Rexfire's secret base, the two members that attacked Prince Lucas had returned, and they told Aria everything, "What!? Why did you do that! Why didn't you fight back!" said Aria, furiously. The research on Rexus had discovered that Rexus had a super attack, that if trained, could destroy the whole castle in minutes, but it would take a while to train up.

Jack, Amy, and Lucas chose that their first places to search would be the Hyperia Plains and the Dunehill Desert, the only desert in Julandia.

Chapter 4

Adventure in the Plains

Jack, Amy, Fluffy and Prince Lucas finally began their quest to find the Seven Keys, with the permission of King Leo, right now, their goal was to head to Dunehill Desert by going through the Hyperia Plains.

"Here's a carrot for you Fluffy!" said Amy, as she was practicing her archery, "No key here!" said Jack, as he was looking for the first key in the set of Seven Keys, Meanwhile, Prince Lucas was reading about the Seven Keys, "Here it says that the seven warriors that created the Seven Keys names were Julian the Warrior, Daria the Merchant, George the Explorer, Sammy the Pirate, Oscar the Craftsman, Niamh the Ninja, and Buster the Blacksmith! Interesting!" said Lucas, "I heard that Julian the Warrior is from Plankteff Town!" said Jack, "Where's that?" asked Amy, "It's just west from here!" said Jack, "I know because I went there with my father a lot, and he said that my mother was from Plankteff Town." said Jack, "How did you lose your mother?" asked Lucas, "My father always said he didn't want to tell me how my mother died, all I really know about her is that her name is Jane Sword and my father's name is John Sword, so because both of their names start with "J" they called me Jack Sword." answered Jack, looking a bit sad now.

"Come on then, I want to see Plankteff Town!" said Amy, "Let's go Jack! Maybe there is someone who knew your mom!" said Lucas, "That's a great idea! Let's go then!" said Jack, who was cheered up.

The group first needed to journey across the Hyperia Plains to arrive at Plankteff Town, and that's what they began to do. "What's your mother like, Lucas?" asked Amy, "I don't see my mother often, even though she is the Queen, she's always on business trips around the kingdom." replied Lucas, "What about your mom, Amy?" asked Jack, "My mother and father live in Shipsail City, a town next to the Splashing Sea, They let me go on this adventure, and shortly after they allowed me I met you, Jack!" said Amy, "Nice!" said Jack. This was a very calm journey, with the sun shining on them, and butterflies and rabbits running all around, the trees were wavering slightly because of the wind, they even saw a nice dog pass by and they all pet it!

Soon though, something interesting happened... Team Rexfire struck again! A chill looking man with a strange hairstyle and a black coat came up to them, "Hey kiddos, what're you doing here! This for Team Rexfire only!" said the strange man, "Go away!" said Jack, "Yeah!" said Lucas, "Oh really, we're doing private business here! We're trying to burn Plankteff Town without little kids messing it up! By the way, the name's Gerry Sledge." said the stranger, "He wants to use fire to burn Plankteff Town! We need to stop him!" said Lucas, "I'll challenge him to a sword battle!" shouted Jack, "I can hear you, you know. I challenge all three of you to battle me one by one, and I'll win each time! Deal?" said Gerry, "Deal." the group replied.

The first battle was decided to be Amy vs Gerry, and Amy left Fluffy on the side-lines and took out her bow, "3, 2, 1, Go!" said Gerry, the battle had begun. Gerry took out a sledgehammer and began to try to crush Amy's bow, and knock it out of her hand! Amy was zooming around the battlefield, looking for a place to aim her bow at the right angle, to shoot Gerry with a flurry of arrows and knock him down, then knock his hammer out of his hand. Amy angled her bow, but it was too late, Gerry had his sledgehammer ready, and he heaved it down and crushed Amy's favourite bow! Amy had lost. She ran back to Fluffy, "Don't worry Amy, I'll beat him for you, then we can get a new bow!" said Lucas, "I have a plan, I will make Gerry dizzy and then forfeit the match, then it's all up to you to finish him off Lucas." said Jack, "Ok!" said Lucas, and then Jack ran over to Gerry.

"My turn!" said Jack, "Come at Me." said Gerry, "Or what about come around me!" said Jack, as he ran around in circles around Gerry, round and round and round, Jerry was spinning too, trying to catch up to Jack, and soon he was very, very dizzy! "Bye!" said Jack, as he switched places with Lucas! Lucas quickly ran over to Gerry and knocked him down with his sword, and then knocked away his hammer with his shield! They had won.

"We won! Gerry, we'll report to the king if you don't stop trying to burn Plankteff Town!" said Lucas, "O-Ok." said Gerry, and he and his small crew ran away. "That was great!" said Jack, "Now we need to get to Plankteff Town to fix my bow, learn about the Seven Keys, and learn about Jack's mother!" said Amy, and so they continued their journey to Plankteff Town.

They continued to walk to Plankteff Town, but then there was another distraction, which was a wild horse! Lucas loved riding horses at the castle, and Amy loved animals, so they all decided to tame the horse.

Lucas ran over to the horse, which was a nice black colour, with a golden mane and lovely blue eyes, it was quite an energetic horse too, "Come here horse!" said Lucas, but the horse just ran away, very, very fast! "Come on!" said Lucas, as he ran and ran, but he couldn't catch up to the horse. The horse looked like it was almost magical, because right when Lucas was about to catch it, it disappeared!

Lucas came back sad, "It's Ok, we don't need a horse, I know a shortcut through Glimmer Forest! We just need to walk a little further! But while they were walking, Lucas saw the horse again, he tried to catch it, but it disappeared again! This happened a third time! But by now they had arrived at the shortcut that Jack was talking about, "We're here!" said Jack.

They walked through the forest for a while, and Lucas tried fresh Glimmer Berries, they continued to walk, and walk, until they saw something very peculiar...

Meanwhile, Team Rexfire were still doing their dangerous business studying the dragon, and Aria was doing something new, learning how to use magic!

Speaking of Magic, the next chapter is all about magic!

Chapter 5

The Fairy Village

Back to Jack, Amy, Fluffy and Lucas, as they were walking through Glimmer Woods, they had found something which they had never seen before! A tiny little village with tiny little fairies, the size of ants!

"Who are you!" asked Jack, "We are the Tini Fairies!" replied the tiny little fairies. "Interesting!" said Lucas, but then they noticed something very, very interesting.

The first key of the Seven Keys was in the centre of the tiny village! "Hey, Tini Fairies, where did you get that giant key?" asked Amy, "It fell from the sky! We love shiny things so we brought it into our village!" said one of the Tini Fairies, who was the leader of them, "Can we have it?" asked Jack, "No! We like it!" replied many Tini Fairies, "What do we do?" asked Jack, "Maybe they will give the key to us if we do things for them!" replied Lucas. "We can't challenge them to a sword fighting duel because they're so tiny!" said Jack, "What if we just stole the key?" suggested Amy, "Good Idea!" said Jack, who was surprised that a sneaky idea like that could come out of Amy's brain!

They were giants to the fairies so they easily just took the key out of the village, and proceeded to just run away, but they wouldn't get a magical artefact that easily, because one of the fairies noticed and blasted a magical beam out of their wand, and shrunk down the group to the size of fairies!

"Get them! They stole the key!" said the leader fairy, and an army of fairies came flying towards them! "We're sorry!" said Lucas, "You see, we're on a quest to stop the kingdom from being destroyed by Rexus!" said Lucas, "We don't care, give us back our key!" said the fairies, "Sorry, is there anything we can do to get your key back?" asked Jack, "There is one thing, can you give us back our shiny pearl?" replied the fairies, "What pearl?" asked Amy, "We used to have a lovely pearl in the middle of the village, but then one day a black bird thought it was its egg and took it away into his nest! He was such a bird-brain!" said the fairies, interestingly still talking in perfect sync.

"Ok then, just tell where the bird went and we'll try to find your pearl!" said Lucas, "The birds nest is right above you! We couldn't get it because the bird would eat us up if we did!" said the fairies, "Really, this is easier than I thought!" said Amy, and she climbed up the brown, tall tree, and when she reached the top of the tree, she saw a little nest with two things in it, a shiny pearl, and a sleeping black crow. "Hey guys, I found the pearl!" said Amy, and Jack, Lucas, and the fairies were watching from below. Amy began to slowly reach out for the pearl, but then the crow sneezed! Amy tried again, this time with the pearl, very slowly, but this time with her broken bow, "Come on Amy!" shouted Jack, impatiently, "Ok, ok just wait a second!" said Amy, but because of all the shouting, the crow woke up! "Caw!" squawked the crow, and then it began to peck Amy!

Amy quickly grabbed the pearl, but the crow began to chase her ferociously! Amy evaded its attacks, and now Lucas and Jack were following Amy! After a few minutes of running away, they looked behind them and saw a whole flock of crows behind them! Jack held them back with his sword, and then they saw a few fairies also holding the crows back!

The crows eventually gave up, and they walked back to the Fairy Village, where the leader fairy welcomed them and said, "First you can give us the pearl, and then we will use a magic spell to shrink you down to our size and you can have a tour of our village, and then we will give you the first key of the Seven Keys, the key of Julian the Warrior, who was one of the warriors who defeated Rexus! Then, the fairies all waved their wands and Jack, Amy, Lucas, and Fluffy, all got shrunk down to about the size of a strawberry!

"Look around!" said the Leader Fairy, "By the way, my name is Freya, Freya the Fairy!" added the Leader Fairy, "Wow!" said Lucas, as he looked at all the mushrooms with doors in them, Meanwhile, Jack rushed to a fairy sword fighting competition, and unfortunately lost against a fairy who was quite skilled at sword fighting. Amy was talking to Freya about the Pearl, "Why do you fairies love that pearl so much?" asked Amy, "The pearl has been in this village for a very long time, and many humans have tried to steal it before, but if they did, we shrunk them down to our size!" replied Freya, "Interesting!" said Amy.

"I guess you may have the giant key now!" said Freya, and the three of them rushed over to the key, "Here you go, you'll be able to hold it when you're big again!" said Freya, "Thank you so much!" said all three of them, "Let's bring them back to normal size!" said Freya, and in a few seconds, they were all back to normal size. The key was in their hands, there was an inscription on the key that said "The key of Julian the Warrior" on it, "Yay!" said Jack, smiling, "We have 1 out of the 7 Keys now!" said Lucas, "Now we can go to Plankteff Town to fix my bow and find out about how Jack's mother died, and then we can head to Dunehill Desert, which is quite a long trip!" said Amy, and so, they continued to trudge through the shortcut in Glimmer Woods, which was called the Glimmer Fairy Path.

The group continued walking, and soon discovered what they were looking for, Plankteff Town! "Let's go!" said Jack, but when they got to the gates of the town, they saw the thing they didn't want to see at all! Three team Rexfire members were standing there, and they immediately saw one of the Seven Keys stick out of Jack's bag! "Hey, give us that key!" said one of them, "Of course not!" said Jack, and he took out his sword, and one of the team Rexfire members did the same!

They both slashed at each other, and Jack used a move that he had learned while fighting of the crows, "Sword Block!" said Jack, and he blocked every single attack with a few flicks of his sword! Then he made a final swoop and beat the member! The three Rexfire members ran away, now they could go into Plankteff.

Chapter 6

Plankteff Town

Jack, Amy, Lucas and Fluffy had arrived in Plankteff Town with one of the Seven Keys in their possession! That day was quite an exciting day for the group, because it was the 10th of April, which meant the annual Spring Festival was going to happen in Plankteff Town, and during the festival Amy was going to get her bow mended, Jack was going to ask around the town about his mother, because she was from Plankteff, and Lucas was just going to enjoy the festival!

First of all, the group walked into the town and decide to split up, "Ok guys, what we're going to do is split up and do the things we want to do, and then we all meet up at the village square at sunset." said Amy, "Ok!" said Lucas and Jack, and the three of them split up. First of all, Amy went to get her bow fixed by the carpenter at the market stalls, as well as to buy more food and supplies, "Hello!" said Amy when she arrived at the stall, "Hello, what do you want?" replied the carpenter, "I would like for my bow to be repaired, please?" replied Amy, "Ok, if you want me to fix your bow, that would cost 3 gold coins and 8 silver coins, do you have enough?" asked the carpenter, "Oh no! I only have 2 gold coins and 4 silver coins! I need 14 more silver coins, or 1 gold coin and 4 silver coins!" said Amy, "We'll then, come back when you have enough." said the carpenter, and Amy left to ask Jack for some money.

Meanwhile, Jack was going around different houses and asking people questions about his mother, Jane Sword, because she was from there and Jack's father didn't want to tell him how his mother died. He knocked on the first door, and a young man with a blonde moustache came out the door, "Hello, have you ever heard of Jane Sword?" asked Jack, "Sorry, I haven't!" the man replied, and he shut the door. Then Jack went to another house, and the same thing happened! He tried one more time, but the same thing happened again! "I give up, so I guess I'll just go and see what Lucas is doing!" thought Jack, but then, Amy came running over to Jack!

"Hello Jack!" said Amy, "Hi, Have you finished getting your bow fixed?" asked Jack, "I was going to, but then I didn't have enough money! I came here to ask you for some!" replied Amy, "How much do you need?" asked Jack, "I need 1 gold coin and 4 silver coins, please!" replied Amy, "Oh no, I don't have enough!" said Jack, "Then let's go and ask Lucas for some, he probably has a lot because he's a prince, right!" said Amy, "Yeah!" said Jack.

They ran around the town looking for Lucas, and after while they finally found him, waiting in a line for some kind of event! "Lucas! What are you waiting here for?" asked Jack, "I'm in line here for a very popular sword fighting competition, it's called The Diamond Dragon Sword Fighting Competition and it happens every Spring Festival here in Plankteff Town! If you win, you get 150 gold coins!" said Lucas, "Wow! That's a lot of money!" said Jack, "If we had that much money, we wouldn't need any more for a very long time! We could even use it to mend my bow very easily!" said Amy, "So we should enter!" said Jack, excitedly, "Oh look, we're almost at the front of the line! There's just one problem, only one of us can enter!" said Lucas, "No problem, all of us can enter separately! Except Amy, of course, because you're not allowed to enter an official tournament if you don't have a sword!" said Jack, "Alright!" said Amy and Lucas.

They got to the front of the line and paid 2 silver coins each for a ticket, and they went into the Diamond Dragon stadium, where there was a massive crowd because of the Spring Festival! They all sat in their seats and watched the first match, which was Mark Slingshot, who looked like the man with the camel that they saw in the castle in New Deyal, versus an unnamed, team Rexfire member!

The two of them charged at each other, and Mark dodged an attack from the Team Rexfire member, and struck back with a strong blow from his copper sword, but all of a sudden, the Team Rexfire member hit Mark's sword, and knocked it out instantly, and it even had a crack in it! The Team Rexfire member let out a merciless laugh, and Mark ran away as fast as he could.

The next match was quite a basic one, and it went quite smoothly, it was a boy with brown hair versus a girl with black hair, and the black haired girl won. The next match was going to be Jack versus a girl called Daisy, and then it would be Lucas versus a boy called Evan. Jack checked how the tournament worked on the poster again, "So first there are sixteen contestants, and I'm one of them, and then there are eight contestants that move on to round 2, then four contestants get to the semi-finals, round 3, and then two people face off in the finals, round four!" thought Jack.

The next match was Jack versus Daisy, and Jack walked onto the Diamond Dragon pitch, which looked very professional. "The next match is between one of last year's semi-finalists, Daisy Heartstrong, versus the newcomer, Jack Sword!" said the judge, and the crowd cheered joyfully, "Ready for this?" asked Daisy, "Yes! What did you expect!" said Jack, "3, 2, 1, Go!" said the judge, and Jack charged at Daisy, but then the unexpected happened, Daisy was just standing there! Jack crashed into Daisy, and then Daisy clashed her sword with Jack's, but Jack didn't give up yet, of course, and with some motivation from Amy, Fluffy, (who squeaked very loudly) Lucas and even Mark, Jack pushed on and a huge clash of swords happened!

The two swords pushed so hard that Amy even saw a few sparks coming off of them! "Come on!" said Jack, "Keep pushing!" said Daisy, and then Jack did something unexpected! Jack quickly stopped pushing his sword and Daisy lost her balance! "Dodge and Slash! Sword Block!" Jack quickly used both moves and knocked Daisy's sword away! Jack got his first win in the Diamond Dragon League!

Chapter 7

The Diamond Dragon League

Jack had just got his first win in the Diamond Dragon League, against Daisy Heartstrong, who ran back to the stands without saying a word.

The next match in the league was going to be Jack's friend Prince Lucas Shield, versus Evan Heartstrong, who was actually Daisy's brother. Jack returned to the stands and Lucas came out onto the pitch, where there were crazy fans screaming at the top of their voice, because Lucas was actually quite a very famous swordsman himself, "Oh yeah, I remember! Lucas was quite good in the stadium in New Deyal, he was even the champion!" said Jack, as he took a seat beside Amy, "Yeah, he's very good!" said Amy, and the match then began.

Lucas easily blocked every single attack that Evan threw at him with his majestic golden shield, with a jewel in the shape of a lion in the middle of it. Lucas's blonde hair blew in the wind, as they heard the chants of the wild crowd. Lucas got knocked down once, but he stood back up extremely fast. Lucas struck again and again, and Evan didn't really know what to do! Evan began to dodge Lucas's attacks and then slashed at him as hard as he could, but then, Lucas jumped high into the air and pointed his sword directly downwards, "Royal Slash!" shouted Lucas as he fell down, then, the pointed edge of Lucas's sword bashed onto Evan's sword, and it went flying across the battlefield until it crashed into a wall.

Lucas had won, and he went back to the stands, with a big smile on his face, bragging to the crowd. Jack went up to him annoyed, "I told you to stop being so overconfident, now you're bragging to the crowd just like you did in New Deyal!" said Jack, "Fine, let me just have some glory this time, I mean didn't you see that awesome new move I just did, it's called Royal Slash!" replied Lucas, and then the next four battles in round 1 took place, and nothing very important happened in those four battles, and now it was round 2, the quarter finals.

First of all, it was the mysterious Team Rexfire member versus Lucas! Last time the Team Rexfire member beat Mark Slingshot very easily! Lucas walked back to the battlefield, and he was still very overconfident from his last battle! The mysterious Team Rexfire member marched over to the battlefield as well, and this was Jack and Amy's first chance to get a good look at him, and he looked scary! She had an eyepatch on her right eye and a large coat of dark blue armour, there was even a rumour amongst the crowd that she had stolen a ticket to get into the tournament! The battle began, and Lucas quickly lashed the Team Rexfire member's sword, but it didn't make a scratch. The Team Rexfire member took out a very dangerous weapon, a double-edged sword! Lucas confidently jumped into the air, "Royal Slash!" said Lucas, but then his sword bounced right off of the Team Rexfire member! Then the Team Rexfire member finally did something, and it was surprising, and against the rules! She lifted up her double-edged sword, and magically lit it on fire! She tried to hit Lucas with it, and the referee tried to stop her but she pushed him away and Lucas had no choice but to forfeit the match.

Again, the Team Rexfire member laughed mercilessly, and returned to the stands. Another match occurred with no problems, and then Jack won his next match! Lastly, the last match in round 2 happened, and now round 3, the semi-finals would happen the next day. While they were walking to their hotel, Jack, Amy, Fluffy and Lucas met Mark! "Hello! Nice to meet you!" said Mark, "Nice to meet you too!" replied Jack, "Sorry about your loss, Prince Lucas!" said Mark, "No problem." said Lucas, and then Mark pet Fluffy while Amy fed her, and by then it was night-time, and they went to bed.

The next day, round 3 began, and the first match was the mysterious villain (which was what they began to call the scary Team Rexfire member) versus another random person called Tommy, and the mysterious villain won easily, again. Then it was Jack versus a person called Ben Dynaboom, and the match ended in another win for him, which meant he was moving on to the finals! "Oh no, I'm really scared now!" said Jack, "It's Ok, I'm sure you'll win!" said Mark, who was beside him.

Round 4, the finals began, and the match was Jack Sword versus the Mysterious Villain. But before the match, the mysterious villain revealed her identity! Jack and the mysterious villain walked over to the battlefield, as the crowd cheered wildly, and that was when the mysterious villain took off her mask, and finally said something!

"Hello, my name is, the one and only, leader of Team Rexfire, Aria Dragonbreath!" shouted Aria, and now it all made sense, Aria had been practising magic, and she learned how to set things on fire using magic! "Oh no..." whispered Jack, and Aria ran straight at him, "You're one of those pests trying to disrupt my plan, aren't you!" said Aria, as she charged, and Jack dodged a fierce attack from Aria and hit back as hard as he could, "Dodge and Slash!" said Jack, and after that he used a Sword Block to deflect one of Aria's attacks! Then Jack decided to repeatedly use both of them at the same time! "Combo Slash!" said Jack, and then he used a new move again, "Mega Force!" said Jack, as he tried his hardest to not only defeat Aria, but also not to get badly injured by her! But it was too late. Jack saw Aria light her sword with a flame of fire! Jack ran away as fast as he could, but Aria decided she didn't need fire, and she put it out and ran straight for Jack! Jack couldn't dodge this time, and his sword went flying out of his hand. He had lost, in a very bad way.

The judge announced that the winner was Aria, sadly, and gave her 150 gold coins, and she left, laughing, but at least Jack won second place, which wasn't actually too bad! He got 50 gold coins, and got a brand new sword, which had a little picture of a dragon on it and the inscription, "Never stop trying" written on it. They went and got Amy's bow fixed, finally, and now it was time to head to the Dunehill Desert, where hopefully they would find the second key, of the Seven Keys!

Chapter 8

The Path to Dunehill Desert

Jack, Lucas, Fluffy, and Amy were all a little bit sad. Jack got second place in the Diamond Dragon tournament in Plankteff Town, and so they raised enough money to fix Amy's bow, and Jack even got a new sword! They were all sad because Jack had lost to Aria, who had learned magic now, in the Diamond Dragon tournament finals! Now that Aria was strong enough, she just needed to wait until Rexus got strong enough to take over Julandia! So now they needed to get the 6 remaining keys in the Seven Keys as fast as they could, and right now they needed to get to Dunehill Desert!

"It's Ok that you lost! At least now we know how strong Aria actually is now!" said Amy, trying to comfort Jack, "Yeah!" said Lucas, but Jack wasn't cheered up, and he didn't say anything, until Mark, from the Diamond Dragon league, showed up, with a camel! Hello you're Majesty Prince Lucas! Hello, I believe your name is Amy Arrow! Hey Jack Sword! Sorry that you lost, anyway, do you need a ride to Dunehill Desert, it can take up to two weeks to get all the way over there from Plankteff!" said Mark, "Yeah! We need to get six more keys!" said Jack, "Oh yes! I've also been looking for one of the Seven Keys, and when I left my home in Cactarab Town in the desert, I thought I saw a gold key in the sand! But then my camel here, Sandie, got frightened by a bushfire and ran away!" said Mark, "So will you give us the ride on your camel?" said Jack, "Only if you beat me in a sword fighting battle!" said Mark, with a smile on his face, and this was when Lucas and Amy realised that this was Mark's plan to cheer up Jack, when Jack won, he would feel happier, and then they would get to Cactarab Town on Mark's camel Sandie! Jack and Mark both took their places, and then Mark took out a nice, copper coloured slingshot! He also took out a few stones to use with the slingshot! Meanwhile, Jack was already feeling happier already! He took out his new Diamond Dragon sword, and the two of them began the battle! "You can't beat me!" said Jack, "Wait until you see my slingshot work!" replied Mark, and Mark pulled back his slingshot's band, and let go! It made a twang sound, "Sandstorm Shoot!" said Mark, and his slingshot released the pebble, and it came flying at Jack!

Jack dodged the attack and ran at Mark, and slashed his slingshot with his sword. Mark lost his grip, but he fumbled around and caught his slingshot before it hit the ground! Mark pulled back the band and used Sandstorm Shoot again, and Jack used a Combo Slash! Then he used a Dodge and Slash and finally used his newest move, Mega Force, in which Jack pushes the opponent as hard as possible to knock away their weapon, and finished the battle, as Mark watched his slingshot drop to the ground.

"I guess we can ride on Sandie to Cactarab Town then!" said Mark, "But how can all five of us fit on one camel?" asked Lucas, "Some people will have to do some sand-surfing then!" said Mark, "What's sand-surfing?" asked Amy, "Sand-surfing is when you put planks of wood on your feet, and then attach a rope to a camel, and hold the other side of the rope! When the camel starts to move, you'll quickly surf along with it!" Mark explained, "Cool!" said Jack, and Jack and Lucas got to sand-surf through the path to Dunehill Desert! Sandie began to move, and Jack and Lucas were slowly surfing along the ground. "Faster Sandie! Faster!" said Mark, and Sandie began to speed up, but they still wouldn't be fast enough until they hit the sand, and eventually, after a day of boring travel, one rest stop, and another boring day of travel (this trip was quite long, it takes one and a half weeks to get from Plankteff Town to Dunehill Desert through the Hyperia Plains) and a few more days of boring travel, they got to the sand, and began speeding very, very fast!

"Woohoo!" said Jack! "This is awesome!" said Lucas, and they zoomed past many, many, cactuses, and that's when they began to notice how hot it was getting! It was sweltering hot, and Jack, Lucas, Amy, and especially Fluffy, who squeaked, tiredly, all felt like they were being baked to a crisp! Meanwhile, Mark was just fine, "Why are you not hot?" asked

Amy, "Because I'm from Cactarab Town! I'm used to these temperatures!" said Mark, "I understand!" said Jack, and they continued to ride through the hot sandy desert. For a second, Lucas thought he had seen the mysterious horse that he saw and tried to catch in the Hyperia Plains, but then it disappeared. Suddenly, a wild sandstorm blocked their vision! They rode on, because they were quite close to Cactarab Town, and then they arrived! Cactarab Town was a market town, filled with merchants, and also thieves! It was a bit dangerous for them, but that was Ok. They stayed in an inn for the night, and woke up the next morning.

Chapter 9

The Pyramid

Jack, Amy, Fluffy, Lucas, and Mark had all arrived at Cactarab Town in Dunehill Desert, because it was speculated that the second key in the Seven Keys, the key of Daria the Merchant, was located in this town!

The group tried looking for the key that Mark had spoken about while they travelled there, but they couldn't find it. "Mark, I think that the key you were talking about isn't real!" said Jack, "Yeah!" said Lucas, "Fine." said Mark, as Fluffy squeaked, but then something crazy happened! A sandstorm began to blow and some sand got into Amy's eyes! "I can't see!" said Amy, as she tried to follow the rest of the group to the inn, and Mark came back to try to help Amy! Mark put Amy onto Sandie and they tried to return to the inn! A few minutes passed and the sandstorm subsided, but then they realised they were in the completely wrong place! They were back in the middle of the desert, and they were lost! Then, they realised another horrible thing! Someone had stolen some of the money kept in Amy's bag! "Oh no!" said Amy, "What?" said Lucas, "25 gold coins are stolen from my bag!" said Amy, "What do we do?" said Lucas, "Look! I think I see the thief running away over there!" cried Jack, and they chased after the thief as fast as they could, with hot sand going into their eyes, and it was hard to run in the hot sun!

They continued to chase the thief until they arrived at his secret base, a giant pyramid! "What in the world!" said Jack, "Let's go inside!" said Lucas, "No! It's dangerous to just happily run into a criminal's hideout!" said Mark, "Well we need to get the money back!" said Lucas, "Our safety is more important than that!" argued Mark, "If our safety was so important, why did we travel through the hot desert with little to no water!" argued Lucas, "Guys, stop fighting!" said Amy, "Yeah, let's just go inside very sneakily, while Mark keeps guard outside!" suggested Jack, "Oh, fine!" said Mark, "Ok" said Lucas, So Jack, Amy, and Lucas went inside the strange pyramid base! It was very spooky inside, and they saw weird markings on the walls! They tiptoed through the base, but then they realised they were lost!

"Where are we?" asked Lucas, "I think I saw this marking before!" said Jack, "I don't remember it at all!" said Amy. Suddenly, they heard a clank sound, and before they knew it, a trapdoor opened underneath them and they were falling down, deep down...

When they finally landed somewhere with a thump, they saw a man wearing a balaclava, a black tunic, and a brown belt! Behind him was a pile of gold, silver, swords, and diamonds! It was all just sitting there, a pile of stolen riches, taller than Jack, Amy, Lucas and Fluffy if they were all standing on top of each other! The man didn't make a sound, instead taking out two small, sharp, swords! "I need to battle him!" thought Jack, and he rushed towards him and used a fierce Combo Slash, just like he had done against Aria in the Diamond Dragon League!

The man quickly dodged the attack, and made his first move, Slashing Jack's sword, leaving a big scrape on it. Lucas joined in too, using his shield to defend Jack, while Amy shot arrows from behind, "Stop it!" was the first thing the man said, but then something caught Jack's eye...

It was one of the Seven Keys! Daria the Merchant's key was right there in the pile! "Lucas, Amy! One of the Seven Keys are in the pile! Lucas, go and get the key!" said Jack, "Yes sir!" said Lucas, and he dived into the pile! But there was a problem! The key was under too much stuff for Lucas to reach! "Jack, Amy! I can't reach the key! I need something small to reach it!" shouted Lucas, "What if Fluffy got the key?" asked Amy, while Jack the Thief fought, "Great Idea!" said Lucas, "Tell Fluffy to come over here!" Lucas added, and Amy told Fluffy to run over to Lucas for a carrot, and Fluffy did!

Lucas told Fluffy to dive into the pile, and she did! Fluffy sniffed around in the pile, got the key, and jumped out! "Yes!

Key No. 2 has been obtained!" said Jack, "But now how do we get out of here, this guy never gives up!" said Amy, "Well maybe he will, if I use Mega Force!" replied Jack, and he used Mega Force and blasted the Thief's swords into the wall! Then they saw a convenient ladder back up to the surface, and got out of the pyramid! They had made it safe and sound, and with the second key in their possession!

Chapter 10

Rodeo Town

Jack, Amy, Lucas and Fluffy had just gotten out of a thief's pyramid base, and they had retrieved the second key in the Seven Keys!

"Mark, look!" said Jack, and Mark turned around from keeping watch outside the pyramid, to see Jack, Amy, Fluffy and Lucas running out of it! Then Mark saw them holding a key! "You guys got another key? Well done!" said Mark, "Yeah! Now we've decided that we're going to start our journey to Rodeo Town to buy supplies!" said Lucas, "Aren't you coming with us, I mean, it would be nice if you joined us in looking for the Seven Keys!" asked Amy, "Of course I am!" said Mark, "Great!" said Jack, "I guess let's start our journey to Rodeo Town then, it's not too far!"

So Jack, Amy, Fluffy, Lucas, and Mark began their journey to Rodeo Town, this time they were on Sandie, with Jack and

Mark on her, while Amy and Lucas were sand-surfing! They trotted onward, and they began to talk about their plans after they were finished in Rodeo Town! "I wonder how we could get the keys a little bit faster, yesterday in Cactarab Town I heard rumours that Aria and Rexus were going to attack pretty soon..." said Lucas, as he surfed on the sand, "I still wish that Aria hadn't cheated in the Diamond Dragon League!" shouted Jack, "I wonder why she was there in the first place!" said Mark, "Maybe she's looking for the Seven Keys too!" said Amy, while feeding Fluffy, "Anyway, back to speeding up finding the keys, Any ideas?" asked Lucas, and everyone thought for a moment. "I know! Why don't we split up!" said Mark, "What do you mean?" said Lucas, "I mean we should split our group up! So me and Amy could go to somewhere, while you two go to a completely different place! That way we could get two keys in the time it takes to get one!" said Mark.

"Great Idea!" said Jack, "Yeah!" said Lucas, "So that's what we're doing after our trip to Rodeo Town!" said Amy, "Yeah, and we've already arrived!" said Jack, and they looked around and saw a town with tumbleweed bouncing through the streets, and horses, or as Mark put it, "There's more horses here than grains of sand in Dunehill Desert!"

There was someone playing a harmonica on a horse, next to someone playing the banjo on another horse! People didn't bother to use their legs here, because they had so many horses! But there was one horse that caught Lucas's eyes immediately, and that was the magical horse from the Hyperia Plains! It was the same black colour, with a golden mane and blue eyes! It was majestically galloping through the desert, and this time Lucas was not going to let that horse go!" It was taunting him, waggling its tail at him! Lucas quickly alerted the others, "Guys, look! It's the horse from before!" said Lucas, "Really? Let's chase it!" said Jack and Amy, "What horse?" Mark said, "I'll explain later, right now, just chase that black horse with us!" said Lucas.

They ran towards the mysterious horse one again, "Pretty ironic that we're having this giant rodeo in a town called Rodeo Town!" thought Jack, as they chased the horse, "I have an idea! Mark taught me about sand-surfing, so what would happen if I surfed on the sand with my shield? I am Prince Lucas Shield, after all!" thought Lucas, so he took out his shield, dropped it onto the floor, and jumped on while he ran, and screamed, "Shield Slide!" The momentum from his running let him slide across the sand easily! Suddenly, while Lucas surfed and Jack and Mark ran, they all heard a cry from Amy, who was at the front of the group, "Guys! I think the horse is stuck! I think it tripped over a tumbleweed and got stuck in quicksand!" said Amy, "Quicksand? I'm rushing over there right now!" said Lucas, and he surfed over to the horse as fast as he could!

When Lucas arrived, the horse was already halfway in the quicksand, and sinking, fast! The others came soon after, "Jack, can you try using Mega Force on the horse?" said Lucas, and Jack tried, but failed, "I can't do that, It would hurt the horse!" said Jack, "I know! I'll use the rope I have, just in case!" said Amy, "Perfect! I'll slide over the quicksand on my shield and tie the rope around the horse, while Jack and Amy hold the rope from the other side! Meanwhile, Mark can use Sandstorm Shoot on the horse to get it to try to pull itself out!" said Lucas, and that's what they did! They all did their jobs, and got the magical horse out!

Chapter 11

The Split Up

Jack, Amy, Lucas, Fluffy, and Mark had all just saved a mysterious horse that they saw for the second time from quicksand! They had all helped to get the horse out, but it was Lucas that the horse seemed to like the most.

"I think we should name him Meteor!" said Lucas, "Why? He doesn't come from outer space or anything!" said Jack, "I don't know, it just feels like the right name! I'm going to try to climb onto Meteor's back now! I've had plenty of horse riding classes back at the castle in New Deyal!" said Lucas, "Oh yes! I almost forgot you were a prince in the first place! Where is your crown?" said Mark, "I only like wearing my crown at public events, I can't just wear a heavy golden crown all the time!" said Lucas, "I guess you can ride on Meteor back to Rodeo Town! We'll go on Sandie!" said Jack. When Jack looked at Sandie, he saw Fluffy all cuddled up fast asleep on

Sandie's hump! "Fluffy sure likes Sandie a lot!" exclaimed Jack.

So they rode back to Rodeo Town, but when they arrived they saw a disaster! It was two team Rexfire agents, wearing black and blue clothes! They were scaring people saying, "Did you know that Aria is almost finished training Rexus, and that she's almost done training herself in magic too! After that, all your precious little horses will be all Aria's!"

"Stop it!" said Jack, "Why should we listen to some kids?" one of the Team Rexfire agents asked, "Because we have two of the - !" said Jack, "Jack, you almost gave away that we have two of the Seven Keys! Good Thing you didn't!" said Amy, "Two of the what?" the agents, "Nothing! But if I beat you in a sword duel, will you stop scaring everyone!" said Jack, "Fine, what about this! We have a showdown tomorrow at high noon, just like how the cowboys do it!" one of the agents said, "Alright, I agree." said Jack, and they went to rest for the next day.

When Jack woke up the next morning, it was already almost noon! He rushed out of bed and got ready, and went to Rodeo Town Square for the duel!

By the time Jack got to the square, his friends were already there waiting for him, and so were the two Team Rexfire agents! "You ready?" one of them asked, "Of course I am!" replied Jack, and they all charged at each other! The Rexfire agents took out two swords and slashed Jack's sword! Jack dashed out a fearless blow, "Combo Slash!" he shouted, as he almost knocked the agents swords out of their hands! But then, suddenly, one of the agents attacked with a really powerful strike of their sword! Jack's sword was just about to drop out of his hand, but then Lucas rushed in on Meteor, and bounced the sword off of his shield, back into Jack's hand, and used a Royal Slash to help! Jack finished off the job with a powerful Mega Force attack that sent the Team Rexfire members running!

Suddenly, the Rodeo Town Mayor arrived at the square, "Thank you so much!" the mayor said, "You're welcome!" said Jack, "I just have one question, why are there so many Team Rexfire members everywhere?" asked Mark, "Yeah!" said Lucas, "I think it's because Aria is looking for the Seven Keys as well! I think she regrets scattering them around the kingdom, and I also think she wants to stop anyone looking for the keys!" the mayor said, "Good thing she doesn't know that we have two of the keys!" Amy whispered to Jack, "Oh don't worry! I already know you have two of the keys! Your secret is safe with me!" the mayor boomed, "Alright, we need to leave now, goodbye!" said Jack, and the group left Rodeo Town.

"So, I guess it's time for us to split up for a bit!" said Mark, "Yeah, so that means me and Lucas will be one pair, and you and Amy will be another pair!" said Jack, "I have no problem with that!" said Amy, "But where will we go?" said Lucas, "Amy and I have already chosen where we're going, the place Amy's parents are from, Shipsail City, next to the Splashing Sea!" said Mark, "Yeah! Where are you two going?" asked Amy, "Oh, we never thought about that, do you have any suggestions?" asked Jack, "Why don't you go to the Maja Jungle? It's not very far from here, unlike our destination!" said Mark, "We'll go there!" said Jack "I guess we're splitting up now! We'll see each other when each pair has a key each, bye!" said Lucas, and they said goodbye, and split up.

Chapter 12

The Wild Road

Jack Sword, Lucas Shield, Amy Arrow, Mark Slingshot, Fluffy, Sandie, and Meteor, had all split up to go to two different places to look for two different keys! On one group there was Jack, Lucas, and Meteor, and on the other group was Amy, Mark, Fluffy and Sandie! Jack, Lucas and Meteor were heading to the Maja Jungle to look for a key, and Amy, Mark, Fluffy and Sandie were heading to Shipsail City to look for theirs!

Just after splitting up, Jack and Lucas rode on Meteor for a little bit, until they reached the path that led to the Maja Jungle, The Wild Road. "The Wild Road? Pretty strange name! This is a pretty normal road to me!" said Jack, "Alright Meteor, let's ride through here!" said Lucas, and Meteor began trotting! "Sometimes I feel like Meteor is doing some sort of magic sometimes!" said Jack, "What do you mean?" asked Lucas, "Sometimes, while Meteor is galloping, when I blink we're in a completely different Place, like Meteor teleported or something!" replied Jack, "I feel that too, but I think it's just because Meteor is so fast!" said Lucas.

"Oh look, it's a monkey!" said Lucas, "Look, it's coming towards us!" said Jack, but then, suddenly, the monkey jumped of the tree onto Jack, and snatched one of the two keys of the Seven Keys Jack had! "Hey! Give that back!" cried Jack, but the monkey jumped back into its tree! Jack jumped off of Meteor and began to climb up the tree, "Give back that key!" shouted Jack, but the monkey just teased Jack as he tried to climb the tall tree!

Suddenly, two people with hats that said "Jungle Explorer" on them, came running to the scene from the jungle, holding boomerangs! "Hello, we heard someone scream and rushed over here as fast as we could! What's the matter?" they asked, "That monkey over there stole one of my keys!" said Jack, "Oh, that's all? You just need to bait the monkey with food, that's all!" they said, and one of them took out a handful of Glimmer Berries and offered them to the monkey, which the monkey accepted, dropped the key, and left.

"Wow! You seem really good with animals!" said Jack, "Yeah!" said Lucas, as Meteor neighed, "Thanks! I'm Richard and she's Bella!" said Richard, "We know the jungle like the back of our hand! Anyway, what are you two kids even doing on the Wild Road? You're really close to the dangerous Maja Jungle..." Bella asked, "We're on a mission to find all of the Seven Keys for the king! It's the only way to stop Rexus!" said

Jack, "How are you sure one of the keys are here?" said Richard, "We're not! We're just looking for it!" said Jack, "Well then we're not letting you into the jungle! It's our duty to keep everyone safe from the Maja Jungle! It's a whole lot different than Glimmer Forest, you know!" said Bella, "I don't get what's so dangerous about the jungle!" said Lucas, angrily, "I'll show you how dangerous it is by telling you the legend that inspired us to start protecting others from Maja Jungle!" said Richard.

It was a quiet summer day in our town, Tangrove Town, and our grandfather had left the town so he could go to Maja Jungle to pick some fruits from the trees! We were just little children at the time, and we waited all afternoon for him to come back, then we waited all evening for him to come back, and even waited all the next morning for him to come back, but he never returned from Maja Jungle. Since then, my sister Bella and I have made it our duty to protect everyone from the dangerous Maja Jungle!" said Richard, "That's a sweet story, but we really need to get into that jungle!" said Jack, "I'm sorry, but we can't let you in." said Bella.

Suddenly, Lucas had an idea! He took his crown out of his bag, placed it on his head, and said in a loud voice, "I, Prince Lucas Shield the First, command you to allow me and my friend to go into the Maja Jungle!" commanded Lucas, "Y-you were Prince Lucas Shield!? Your majesty, we will gladly allow you and your acquaintance to enter Maja Jungle!" said Richard, "You don't have to act all posh around me, I already saw how you really act!" laughed Lucas, "Alright, just go into the jungle, just don't blame us if you get hurt or lost!" said Bella, and they continued past Bella and Richard along the Wild Road, and entered the Maja Jungle.

When they got into the jungle, it started lashing rain and thunder, which was scaring Meteor! After a few minutes, they got lost. Now this would be a wild ride....

Chapter 13

Whirlwind Canyon

While Jack, Lucas and Meteor were on the Wild Road, Amy, Mark and Fluffy were riding northwest on Sandie, back through the Dunehill Desert and Hyperia Plains to Whirlwind Canyon, the passageway to their destination, Shipsail City.

They were riding on Sandie, when Amy said this, "Look! I can see Whirlwind Canyon! I used to go there all the time when I was younger! There's even a river that leads to a waterfall that I love!" said Amy, "It's a bit too windy for my tastes!" said Mark. Whirlwind Canyon was a windy, mountainous place with a river cutting through it, which went past to a waterfall called Whirlwind Falls, which went down a huge cliff, with Shipsail City and the Splashing Sea at the bottom.

"Oh Look! I think that there's a boat service over there!" said Mark, "Yeah! But how will we get Sandie on a boat?"

asked Amy, "We'll just have to rent an extra big one!" said Mark, "Ok!" said Amy, and by then they had arrived at Whirlwind Canyon.

When they arrived at the river through Whirlwind Canyon, they saw a shady looking man beside a big boat that looked like it was made a hundred years ago! It was cracked, and clearly looked like it had been quickly patched up many times, and the wood on the boat was so old it was a pale, brownish green! "Are you sure we should take this boat?" Amy asked, as she pointed to a gigantic golden ship, "Wow! Let's take that ship instead!" said Lucas, and they went over to the ship.

When Lucas and Amy got to the ship, they saw a nice looking man at the door! "How much gold does it cost to take this ship to Shipsail City?" Lucas asked to the man, "45 gold coins and 5 silver coins will do!" the man replied, "We only had 130 gold in total, and we split that up to 75 gold for each group! If we pay almost 46 gold that's most of our money gone!" said Lucas, "I guess that means we're not taking the ship..." said Amy, sadly, and they returned to the old, broken, boat.

At the old boat, Lucas asked how much gold it would be to take the boat, "Only 8 silver coins! 2 silver coins as a tip would be nice too!" the man said, "It's a great deal! You get to experience the smaller, more exciting and dangerous river instead of the boring old regular one, there's even a waterfall on the path I use for my customers!" the man said, "Ok, we'll rent it!" said Lucas, and they took the boat.

First of all, Lucas got into the boat, and it shook a little when he got in! Then, Amy and Fluffy got into the boat, and again, it shook a little!" Lastly, Sadie got into the boat with the help of Lucas, and the boat almost sank when Sandie got in! Lucas and Amy started paddling through the river, and soon realised what the man had meant when he said "You get to experience the smaller, more exciting river!" Lucas and Amy had to paddle through countless intense currents, a lot of twists and turns, Lucas got seasick, and a fish even jumped into their boat! It was a disaster!

"Now I really wish we had taken the expensive ship..." said Lucas, "Yeah..." said Amy, "You know, we've been rowing for ages! How come we still haven't seen Whirlwind Falls?" asked Amy, "Wait, why do I see the river going down over there... Do you think – No, it can't be!" said Lucas, "What!?" asked Amy, "Do you think that we're heading straight down the waterfall soon?" asked Lucas, "Oh no, I think so!" said Amy, "Don't panic, its fine, don't panic!" Lucas told himself, "What do we do? We're heading for a waterfall!" screamed Amy, "I have an idea! Amy, take out that rope you have for emergencies! The one you used to save Meteor from quicksand!" said Lucas, "Ok! Now what?" asked Amy, "Ok, now lasso the tree with the rope, that way the boat will get caught by the rope if we hold onto it, stopping us from falling down the waterfall! Then we can jump of the boat and swim to land!" said Lucas, and that's what they did! Amy lassoed the tree to stop them from moving, and they jumped off the boat with Fluffy and Sandie to safety!

"You know what, I think that man who offered us this boat was probably a Team Rexfire member trying to get rid of us!" said Lucas, "Yeah!" said Amy, and they travelled to Shipsail City.

Chapter 14

The Majaful Tribe

While Mark, Sandie, Fluffy and Amy were at Shipsail City, Jack, Lucas and Meteor were lost in the jungle, just like Bella and Richard had said happened to their grandfather!

Jack, Lucas and Meteor were all terrified by the creepiness of the Maja Jungle, with bugs that were the size of dogs, trees taller than Jack and Lucas had ever seen, and rain that lashed down for ages, and then stopped for a few minutes, and started lashing again! These conditions were the best conditions for get lost in, and so, they were lost.

Jack and Lucas continued riding on Meteor. They had been riding, searching for any keys, and resting for two days now, and they were tired, and covered with mosquito bites. As they continued riding Meteor, Jack heard some rustling in the bushes! "What's that?" said Jack, "What?" shouted Lucas, and that triggered the best in the bushes to jump out! "It's one of those forest monsters!" said Jack, "What forest monsters?" said Lucas, "Once, in me and Amy encountered a weird forest monster in Glimmer Forest! Quick throw some berries at it!" said Jack, "Why?" said Lucas, "You need to because Amy taught me that you calm these down by giving them food!" said Jack, "Ok!" said Lucas, and he threw a Glimmer Berry at the beast. The forest beast took the berry and ran away.

"Phew! That was a close one!" said Jack, "Wait, I hear people chanting!" said Lucas, "Yeah!" said Jack, "They're talking in some foreign language!" said Lucas. They peeked through the bushes, and saw some kind of tribe chanting, "Majaful! Majaful! Majaful! Tribool! Majaful! Majaful! Majaful! Tribool!" the tribe chanted, "Who are they?" asked Lucas, "Don't know, but look what the chief is holding up!" said Jack, "Is that one of the Seven Keys?!" asked Lucas, "I think it is! The key of George the Explorer!" said Jack, "We need to get in there right now!" said Lucas, "I don't think we can though, they seem to really, really like that key, I mean they're literally chanting and partying for this key!" said Jack, "Come on Jack, the whole reason we journeyed through the jungle for days is so we could get this key!" said Lucas, and he jumped over the bush with his sword in his hand!

"I guess were taking the surprise attack approach then!" said Jack, and he jumped over the bushes too! The tribe were at first confused, until Jack snatched the key off of their chief saying, "Sorry, but we really need this!" Suddenly, the tribe reacted by taking out lit torches and started trying to hit Jack and Lucas, "Dodge and Slash!" said Jack, and he slashed his sword, and they fought the tribe!

Suddenly, Jack and Lucas heard a loud voice, "What are you doing to the tribe! Go away!" an old man said, running towards them, "Wait, are you Bella and Richard's grandfather?" asked Jack, Suddenly, the old man froze, and tears came to his eyes, "I-I haven't heard my grandchildren's names in years! Who-o are you?" he said, with tears of joy, and Jack and Lucas explained everything, about how Bella and Richard were guarding the jungle, and how they were looking for the Seven Keys, all during the chaos of the battle!

"Bella and Richard are still waiting for me? I thought they would have forgotten about me long ago! When I got lost in the Maja Jungle, this tribe kindly sheltered me! But now I must leave right away! Come on, bring the key and run! I want to see my grandchildren right now!" the old man said, and so they ran, and ran, and ran! They escaped the Majaful Tribe, ran past a giraffe, elephant, and tiger! (Which made them run even faster) They ran all day, and then luckily reached the edge of the jungle! When Bella and Richard came into sight, their grandfather was crying with joy, and almost tripped over! Suddenly, they heard Bella scream, "Richard! Grandpa's here! GRANDPA'S HERE!" and their grandfather ran the fastest he'd ever ran, and hugged his two grandchildren, and all of them were both laughing and crying! All Bella and Richard managed to say was, "Thank you Jack and Prince Lucas, for making our family happy again!"

"What a day!" said Jack, "We got the third key, and we brought Bella and Lucas's grandfather back!" said Lucas, "I guess it's time for us to head to Shipsail City, to see how Amy and Mark are doing!" said Jack, "Yes! I can't wait to tell them all about this journey in the jungle!" said Lucas.

Chapter 15

The Pirates

While Jack, Lucas and Meteor were in the Maja Jungle hunting for the third key, Amy, Mark, Fluffy and Sandie were looking for the fourth key in Shipsail City!

"Good thing we got away from the Whirlwind Falls before we fell down it!" said Amy, as they approached Shipsail City, "Look! We're here!" said Lucas, happily, and they walked into Shipsail City! The place was filled with ports and bays, with fishermen everywhere! There was a bright blue open sky, with seagulls flying through it! There was even a lovely view of the beach and the sea, and Mark and Amy admired it!

Suddenly, Amy pointed at a ship in the bay and said, "That's my dad's ship! My dad's job is to stop pirates from getting into the waters between Shipsail City and the Island of New Sealand!" said Amy, "Where's New Sealand?" asked Mark, "New Sealand is an island at the southernmost point of

Julandia!" replied Amy, as she fed Fluffy, "Let's go to your dad's ship once I leave Sandie at that guy's horse stable over there!" said Mark.

So Mark left Sandie at the stable, and once he'd done that. Mark and Amy went over to the bay. When they got to the bay, Amy said hello to her dad, who was standing there! "Hello, sweetie!" Amy's dad said, in a raspy voice, "Hello dad!" said Amy, "How have your adventures been going, have you sailed the sea yet?" Amy's dad asked, "No dad, I was hoping me and my new friend Mark could sail to New Sealand today! I also have two other friends called Jack and Lucas, but they're searching for a key in the Maja Jungle!" said Amy, "No problem! I was going to sail to New Sealand anyway, it's no big deal bringing two extra crew members on board! Amy, you can raise the sail, and Mark, you stay on the lookout for pirates!" Amy's dad said, "Aye Aye, Sir!" said Mark, "Well then, let's get going!" Amy's dad said.

So they boarded Amy and her dad's ship! Lucas climbed a ladder up to the top of the mast, to lookout for pirates, Amy raised the sail, and they began sailing! The seas were calm, with a nice breeze blowing through the sea, and there were no pirates! Everything seemed to be going well, until...

Dark clouds began to set in, and they heard the boom of thunder, the wind began to blow much harder, and they heard Mark scream from up above, "PIRATES!!!" and suddenly, they saw a cannonball barely miss their ship! "You're right Mark. Pirates!" Amy's dad shouted, "Ready the cannons!" one of the crew said, and then the pirate ship came into view! These were no ordinary pirates, they were Team Rexfire Pirates! Suddenly, Amy noticed them flaunting one of the Seven Keys at them!

"Mark! Look, they've got the fourth key!" shouted, as the stormy sea rocked the boat, and rain lashed down on them,

"Oh yeah! We need a plan to get it!" said Mark,

"And I think it involves my trusty rope!" said Amy, as Fluffy quivered with fear, and Amy's dad fired cannons! Suddenly, Amy had the craziest idea! She took her rope and threw one end of the rope, holding the other, and lassoed it onto the mast of the pirate ship! Now there was a clear tightrope between the two ships!

"Amy, what are you doing, that's too dangerous!" Amy's dad said, but Amy had already left Fluffy on deck and went on the rope! Amy carefully tiptoed across the rope, as everyone watched in awe! Amy's dad was very, very, worried, and then, he saw one of the pirates take out their sword! They were going to cut Amy's rope! "Amy, Jump!" Amy's dad shouted, and Amy jumped just in time, just as the rope was cut!

"Goodbye, my trusty rope" Amy said, as she jumped onto the pirate ship, with her bow ready! An epic clash occurred, and Amy fought with all her might, but then, suddenly, two pirates caught her by surprise! The last thing she managed to do before she got tied up was to throw the fourth key, the key of Sammy the Pirate, which she had gotten from the pirates during the battle, onto her dad's ship! Then Fluffy and her were tied up by the pirates to a post, and taken away on their ship to their base in New Sealand!

"We've got the fourth key, but we haven't got Amy! What do I do?" thought Mark, "We have to save her!" Amy's dad said, worriedly, "I know what to do! We need to send a letter to Jack and Lucas so they can help us!" said Mark, and he quickly wrote a letter, saying,

"Dear, Jack and Lucas, I've found the fourth key, but I've lost Amy! Come to Shipsail City, now..."

Chapter 16

Amy is in Danger!

When Jack and Lucas received the letter from Mark, they were almost at Whirlwind Canyon, not too far from Shipsail City!

Jack and Lucas were camping at Whirlwind Canyon, when they saw a messenger on a horse, holding a letter! "Who sent us a letter?" asked Jack, "It's probably Mark or Amy, let's see what they wrote! And Lucas too the letter from the messenger and said "Thank you!" and the messenger left. "Open the letter!" said Jack, "Ok!" said Lucas, and he opened up the letter, and they both read it, and it wrote,

To,

Jack Sword and Prince Lucas Shield,

"Dear, Jack and Lucas, I've found the fourth key, but I've lost Amy! Come to Shipsail City, now! Amy has been captured by pirates and brought to the Island of New Sealand! Amy's parents, Mr. and Mrs. Arrow are with me, and we need your help! Pease come over to Shipsail City as soon as possible!

Signed,

Mark Slingshot

"Oh no! We need to get to Shipsail City as fast as we can! Come on, let's go!" said Jack, and he began running as fast as he could! "Why don't we just ride Meteor?" asked Lucas, "Oh yeah, Good Idea." said Jack as he rushed to their camp!

About an hour or two later, Jack and Lucas reached Shipsail City and dropped off Meteor at the stable, and Mark and Amy's dad came as fast as they could and told them everything! "Amy is captured by pirates and taken to Shipsail City? Come on, we need to go right away!" said Jack, and they quickly hopped aboard Amy's dad's ship and began sailing!

"So, you found the third key!" said Mark, "Yeah!" said Jack, as they sailed, and Jack and Lucas told the story of how they got a key to Mark, and to Amy's father! After that, they had almost arrived at the island of New Sealand! "New Sealand is the most recently discovered place in Julandia! It's also known for its beaches, and turtles roaming the island!" Amy's dad said, "Interesting!" said Lucas, "I'm surprised that Amy became friends with the Prince of Julandia, and never told me!" Amy's dad said.

Soon, they arrived at New Sealand, and they got off of the ship and began searching for the pirate's base! "Where is the Team Rexfire Pirate's base?" asked Jack, "I don't know, but we've got to keep searching!" Amy's dad said, "Look over here guys! I think I've found the pirates base!" shouted Mark, "Really, where?" asked Lucas, "Over here!" replied Mark, and they all ran over to where Mark was, and they all peeked through the bushes, to see a medium sized building, with the Team Rexfire flag waving at the top!

"Come on, let's go inside!" whispered Lucas, and they quietly snuck inside of the pirate base! They heard pirates talking, saying, "We've stolen all the girl's money, and her rabbit! Now what do we do to her?" a pirate said, "They've stole all of Amy's money, and Fluffy!" whispered Jack, as they crept through the pirate base, and then, suddenly, they saw Amy, still all tied up in one of the rooms! "Jack? Lucas? Mark? Dad? Is that you?" Amy asked, "Yes, it's us! We've come to save you!" Amy's dad whispered, as he untied the rope around Amy, "Oh yes, oh yes! Thank you! Now we just need to save Fluffy!" shouted Amy, and that alerted the pirates!

"Who's there?!" one of the pirates grumbled, "Oh no!" shouted Jack, and all of the pirates charged into the room! Jack and Lucas quickly took out their swords! "I've been practicing this in secret for a while! Watch!" said Jack, and he began spinning around quickly with his sword out! "Spinning Slash!" shouted Jack, as he struck as he spun! Meanwhile, Lucas was also skilfully handling the pirates! Amy was helping out too, gracefully using her bow to distract the pirates, and knocking one of their swords away! Meanwhile, Mark had an idea! While the pirates were distracted by all the commotion, Mark snuck into the room with Fluffy and the money was in! He took them back easily, and headed out, shouting, "Everyone! I've got all of our things! We can run away now!" shouted Mark.

Jack, Lucas, Amy, Fluffy, Mark, and Amy's dad all hopped onto the ship, and escaped from the island of New Sealand, and returned to Shipsail City, with four keys!

Chapter 17

The Letters

Jack, Lucas, Amy, Fluffy, Mark, and Amy's dad had all just escaped from the pirates on the island of New Sealand, and now they were back at the bay of Shipsail City!

Jack and Lucas were practicing their sword-fighting skills by duelling against each other, while Amy, Mark, Fluffy, and Amy's dad were enjoying lunch! Meteor and Sandie were still at the nearby stable! While all this was happening, the messenger went over to Jack, Lucas, Mark, Amy, Fluffy, and Amy's dad! "I have some letters for you, again!" the messenger said, and he handed Jack four letters, and then left! "More letters, cool! Let's see the first one!" said Jack, "Come on, show us!" said Amy, as Fluffy squeaked, and Jack opened up the first scroll, "This one's for me!" said Jack, and the letter wrote,

To,

My son Jack Sword,

Hello, Jack, I've just wrote this letter to make sure you're fine and safe! It's been quite a while since you left in the spring, now its late autumn! Again, I hope you're doing well! I've heard that you've become friends with Prince Lucas the First! That's great! I've also heard some rumours that you've already found four of the Seven Keys! If that's true, please write back to me! However, there's a small problem, there are also rumours that Aria has almost fully trained and strengthened Rexus, so the key hunters must speed up! One last thing, I have something very, very important to tell you! If you want to hear it, send a letter back so I know you're well.

From,

Mr. Sword (your dad).

Jack read it all out loud, "I need to hear the important thing! Let me write my response right now!" Jack said, as he gave the other three letters to Lucas, "Ok, I'll open the next one!" said Lucas, and he opened the next one, and it wrote,

To,

Mark Slingshot,

Mark Slingshot, your registered horse and camel have been causing trouble at the Official Horse Stable of Shipsail City, can you please come and collect them. Sorry if this is an inconvenience for you, we hope you come soon, Have a good day.

From,

Roger Saddleman at the Official Horse Stable of Shipsail City.

"Hey, you registered Meteor using my name?" said Mark, "Yes, sorry!" said Lucas, "But you're Prince Lucas, you don't need to do any of that!" said Mark, "Oh yeah, I've been away from the castle for so long that sometimes I forget that, "Anyway, I'm going to go and pick up Meteor and Sandie! And Mark went to pick up Meteor and Sandie!

Lucas opened up the next letter, which was a lot fancier than the other ones! "Let me guess, this is from my dad, King Leo!" said Lucas, and the letter wrote,

To my son, Prince Lucas Shield the First,

Greetings, Lucas, I have an important thing to tell you! A messenger just came, and told me that Aria has almost restored Rexus to its full power! This means that everyone searching for the keys must speed up! I wrote to tell you that! Your mother is missing you quite a lot, so it would be nice if you would write to her. I hope you are doing well.

From,

King Leo Shield the Third.

"I'm going to write to my mother right away!" said Lucas, "Amy, you can read the last letter, me and Jack are listening!" said Lucas, "Ok, this last one is from a stranger!" said Amy, and the letter wrote,

To,

Jack Sword, Prince Lucas Shield the First, and a few others,

Hello, key hunters, I've written this letter to tell you that I believe I have found one of the Seven Keys! It's in my possession right now! I would appreciate it if you came to Mystical Village, through the Foggy Fields as soon as possible. Thank you for reading.

From,

Kyle the Wizard.

"Woah! A wizard has the fifth key? I wonder if he'll teach us any magic, I mean if Aria could use it, we could use it too!" said Jack, Suddenly, Mark arrived with Sandie and Meteor and said, "I heard everything, come on, Mystical Village is pretty far, so let's take Amy's dad's ship! "Great idea!" Amy's dad said, and Amy said goodbye to her mother, Jack and Lucas dropped of their response letters, and the whole group got into Amy's dad's ship.

Chapter 18

Foggy Fields

Jack, Lucas, Amy, Mark, Amy's dad, Fluffy, Sandie, and Meteor were all in Amy's dad's ship, on their way to Foggy Fields, because a wizard called Kyle had wrote a letter to them, saying that he had the fifth key, and that they had to go to Mystical Village, through Foggy Fields, to meet him.

"I'm so happy to see you again Meteor!" said Lucas, "Same to you, Sandie!" said Mark, as they sailed, "You know, I really hope this wizard is telling the truth, we need to find the rest of the keys as fast as we can!" said Jack, "Yeah!" said Amy. After around two and a half hours of travelling, they finally arrived! They got out of the ship and immediately saw a huge area full of thick fog right ahead of them! "How are we supposed to see in there?" asked Jack, "I don't know!" said Mark, "Maybe if we just ride straight as fast as we can, we'll just reach the end of the fog!" Lucas suggested, "Why is everything so, you know, perfectly named! A town full of horses was called Rodeo

Town, a city full of ships was called Shipsail City, and now a field full of fog is called Foggy Fields!" thought Mark.

"Amy, I'm sorry but I need to go now, it was really nice seeing you again!" Amy's dad said, and Amy went and hugged her dad saying, "Goodbye dad!" and Amy's went back to the ship and returned to Shipsail City.

"Alright, now it's time to head into the Foggy Fields!" said Jack, "But how will we see through all that fog?" asked Amy, "We should just march straight through it!" said Lucas, "Ok, so we should just march through the fog, it can't go on for too long, right?" said Jack, and they all began to walk through the fog! They couldn't see a thing, so they often bumped into something or tripped over something! Sometimes, they would see little flashes and sparkles flying about, and they even saw a fairy fly past! It looked like one of the Tini Fairies from Glimmer Woods! Meteor seemed to be loving the place, prancing ahead of everyone, while Sandie seemed to not enjoy the place as much, lagging behind. After a while, he fog began to clear, and that's when they saw how beautiful the place actually was!

There were shimmering lights and pretty flowers everywhere! There were a lot of cats and kittens running around, and the whole place looked stunning! "Wow!" said Jack, "Look, I'm petting one of the kittens!" said Amy, joyfully! They decided to stop and relax for a while, and they ate dinner, and then set up camp and slept there.

The next morning, they all woke up and ate breakfast, and then started moving again! The fog started to set in again, and once more they couldn't see a thing! They continue to hike up a big hill, and when they reached the top they were above the fog! They looked down and saw the majestic Mystical Village below them! It had funnily shaped houses, and there was a nice lake in the middle of the village!

They went down the hill into the village, and it looked very magical! More fairies were flying around, and everyone walking around the village was holding wands! One lady waved her wand at a bare tree, and shouted some nonsense words, and then leaves and apples appeared on the tree! Another person was using their wand to count their money! One man was even using his wand to turn a cat into a dog, and then back into a dog again! "I wonder where this wizard is, everyone here looks like a wizard!" said Lucas, and then Jack pointed at a house at the top of a hill, "Maybe it's that one!"

They walked over to the hill, ad climbed up to the funny looking house at the top of the hill! It looked like it was a mushroom that was about to topple over! It had a blue roof and white walls, and there was a ginger cat standing outside the house!

They could hear a cauldron bubbling from the inside, and they heard the sounds of sparks flying! "This guy seems a little crazy!" said Amy, "Yeah, definitely!" said Mark, and then, just as Jack was about to knock on the door,

they heard a big, "BOOM!"

and they heard, "Oh no! The last ingredient!"

then, Jack knocked on the door, and then the wizard on the inside said,

"Oh no! They're here already! Too late to find it now!"

and he opened the door, and Jack, Amy, Lucas, Mark, Fluffy, Meteor and Sandie all saw...

Chapter 19

Kyle the Wizard

They all saw a very strange wizard! He was wearing a purple robe, and was holding a wand in his hand, which had a pearl at the end of it! At the inside of the strange house, there was a bubbling cauldron, and it was very messy!

"Hello, hello! I see you got my letter! I am Kyle the Wizard!" said Kyle, "Yes, we know! So, you claim to have the fifth key in your possession?" said Jack, "Yes! I do, but before I give it to you, I need to ask you for a little help!" said Kyle, "What do you need help with?" asked Amy, "Recently, I've been working on a potion that can calm down wild Grumbors!" said Kyle, "What are Grumbors?" asked Lucas, "Grumbors are wild beasts that have three eyes, and sharp teeth! They live in forests and jungles!" said Kyle, then, Jack, Amy, and Lucas looked at each other! "Our group has had two encounters with those before!" said Jack, "Oh really! They're really dangerous! Anyway, I've been working on a potion that calms them down!

I've got a bunch of ingredients, like soothing salty seawater from Shipsail City, the leaves of a Calmingo Tree, and even a little bit of fairy dust! But every time I try feeding this potion to a Grumbor, it doesn't work! Do you guys have any suggestions?" asked Kyle.

"Wait! I know! Each time we encountered a Grumbor, we calmed I down using Glimmer Berries! I have some here!" said Jack, "When did you guys ever meet a Grumbor?" asked Mark, "I'll tell you later!" said Jack, "Glimmer Berries! That's a great idea! Can you drop two Glimmer Berries into the cauldron?" asked Kyle, "Sure!" said Jack, and he dropped two Glimmer Berries into the cauldron! It crackled a little, and changed into a bluish colour!

"It looks great! Thank you so much! I'll test it later!" said Kyle, "No problem! Just one thing, before you give us the fifth key, can you lease teach us a magic spell that we can do without a wand?" asked Mark, "Well, you need to be incredibly good at magic to do any spells without a wand, even I can't do that! However, you can do the most basic spell without a wand!" said Kyle, "What's that?" asked Jack, "It's a simple spell that lets you create fog around you! It's called the Basic Vanishing Spell! It's always the first spell anyone trying to learn magic learns!" said Kyle, "So how do you do it?" asked Mark, "First you must put both of your hands on your head!" said Kyle, and they all did that, (except for the pets of course) "Now whisper this out loud, "Foggius Summonus!" said Kyle, and they all whispered, "Foggius Summonus!" and fog came all around each one of them, except Lucas!

"Hey, why didn't it work for me?" asked Lucas, "Did you truly believe the magic would work?" asked Kyle, "I think I did?" said Lucas, "Try again!" said Kyle, and Lucas tried again, "Foggius Summonus!" and it worked! Smoke filled the room and everyone was happy! "Woohoo!" said Lucas, and then, Kyle took a key out of his hat! Here you go! I found the fifth key while I was testing my potion recipe! "Thank you so much!" said Jack, "Now we have the fifth key!" said Lucas, and now they had the key of Oscar the Craftsman! Suddenly, they heard a knock on the door!

They saw another person bringing a letter! "Who could it be for this time?" asked Mark, "Maybe it's a response letter for me, from my dad!" said Jack, and the delivery man handed the letter to Jack, and left. Jack opened up the scroll, and read the letter!

As Jack read, he seemed like he was shock about something! His eyes were wide open, and he was even shivering a little bit! When Jack finished reading the letter, he froze in shock! "Jack? What's the matter?" asked Amy, and she took the letter and read it! Here's what it said,

To,

Jack Sword, my son.

Dear Jack, you wrote back to me saying whatever the important thing was, you were ready to hear it. You really are brave! Anyway, here's what you need to know. When you were just two years old, I told you that your mother had died!

However, she had actually never died! She had been captured by Rexfire ninjas when you were very young, and I told you that she died so that you wouldn't go off and try to save her, because if you did when you were so young, that would be dangerous! So, I want you to go and save her! The ninjas and your mother are at Combaido City, Not too far from Mystical Village!

From,

Mr. Sword, your dad.

Chapter 20

Bamboozen Forest

"No way! Jack's mum is alive?!" said Lucas, "I-I can't b-believe this! This m-must be a d-dream!" marvelled Jack, "Thank you so much for giving us the fifth key, but we need to head to Combaido City right away!" said Mark, "Yeah!" said Amy, "No problem! To get to Combaido City you need to go through Bamboozen Forest! But before you go, let me brew up a speed potion for your horse and camel to drink! It'll make them much faster!" said Kyle, "Ok, thank you so much!" said Lucas.

Then, Kyle went to his brewing station, and boiled some water, and then dropped what looked like sparks of lightning into the water! The water frizzled, and finally, Kyle dropped some Lokobi Berries into the mixture! "Lokobi Berries! I have faint memories of my mom giving one to me! I'm so excited to save my mom!" said Jack, "Lokobi Berries are more sour than

Glimmer Berries, but they are really good for you!" said Mark, and then, the potion was done!

Kyle gave it to Amy, "Thank you for the speed potion, and thank you so much for the fifth key!" said Amy, "No problem, now you should get going, Jack must save his mother!" said Kyle, "It's time to save my mom!" shouted Jack, and they gave the speed potion to Meteor and Sandie, and then Jack, Amy, Fluffy, Lucas, Mark, Sandie, and Meteor said goodbye to Kyle, and rode away from Mystical Village, to save Jack's mom!

"I'm so excited!" said Jack, "Yeah!" said Lucas, "We have five out of seven keys now, so that means we only need two more!" said Mark, "Wow! Meteor and Sandie are going so fast!" said Mark, "Yeah! I still feel that strange teleportation thing whenever I ride Meteor!" said Lucas, "Me too!" said Jack, and then they continued down the path, until they reached Bamboozen Forest, a forest filled with bamboo, and pandas!

The sun was out, and there was a lovely breeze blowing as they rode! They saw pandas, eating bamboo, and Amy even pet one of the baby ones! "Wow! This is a calming, wonderful place!" said Amy, "Yeah, it's a great place, but I don't feel calm at all, I'm about to rescue my mom, after not seeing her for ten years! I don't even remember what she looks like!" said Jack, "How are you supposed to save her if you don't remember what she looks like?" asked Mark, "I don't know, but I'm sure my mom would look sort of like me!" replied Jack,

"Look everyone, I see somebody standing straight ahead!" said Lucas, "Who could that be?" thought Jack, and as they rode ahead, they noticed that the person standing there was an old lady, wearing a Team Rexfire outfit!

"What? How can somebody so old be part of Team Rexfire?" asked Amy, "Don't know, but whoever it is, she's clearly trying to block us!" said Lucas, "Wait, she looks familiar to me for some reason!" said Jack, "What do you mean?" asked Mark, "She looks exactly like Mrs. Rita!" said Jack, "Who's Mrs. Rita?" asked Lucas, "She's a cranky old lady who lived in Lighton Village, where I'm from!" said Jack, "Well, young Jack Sword, It appears that you recognize me, Mrs. Rita!" said Mrs. Rita, "Yes, but why are you wearing Team Rexfire clothes?" asked Jack, "Don't you understand, Jack? I've been a Team Rexfire secret agent the whole time! I was sent to make sure your dad didn't try to save your mom! Recently, I've heard you're going to save her, and it's my duty to stop you from saving your mom!" said Mrs. Rita, "No way! I'm challenging you to a sword duel!" shouted Jack, angrily, and they both charged at each other, with their swords out! "Mega Force!" shouted Jack, as he blasted Mrs. Rita back 5 meters! "Hey, respect your elders, young man!" tutted Mrs. Rita, and they clashed their swords, "Heh, I've been practising this, Spinning Slash!" shouted Jack, and he spun round and round, until he knocked Mrs. Rita's sword away! "Hey, my old hands were shaking, that's not fair!" said Mrs. Rita, "It was fair and square!" shouted Jack, "Arrgh!" shouted Mrs. Rita, as she ran away!

The group kept moving through Bamboozen Forest, petting pandas, and looking at the lovely bamboo! They continued riding, until it was night time! When it was the night, and they were about to start camping, they noticed some beautiful red lanterns ahead! "We must be close to Combaido City! Let's keep moving until we arrive there!" said Jack, and they kept riding Meteor and Sandie, until they reached Combaido City!

Chapter 21

The Glowing Festival

Jack, Amy, Mark, Lucas, Fluffy, Sandie, and Meteor had all just arrived in Combaido City, to save Jack's mom! "Look at all of these lanterns in the sky!" said Jack, "Oh yes! Tonight is the Glowing Festival! It's a festival that happens exactly one week before the end of autumn!" said Mark, "Yes! It's a festival that represents hope, even in hard times! All the lanterns in the sky are to remind people that even when they're going through tough times, they always have hope!" said Lucas.

Suddenly, they saw a girl running towards them, and a few seconds later she crashed into them! "Sorry!" she said, "Wait! What are you running away from?" asked Jack, "I was running away from the Team Rexfire Ninja Base!" the girls said, and the Jack noticed she was wearing a Team Rexfire outfit! "You seem a little too young to be part of Team Rexfire!" said Jack, "Well, I guess I have to introduce myself, I'm Nina Katana, a Team Rexfire Ninja trainee! I don't really like Team Rexfire though!" said Nina, "If you don't like team Rexfire, then why are you training to become part of them?" asked Amy, "My mom and dad are part of Team Rexfire, and I've been part of Team Rexfire since I was born!" said Nina, "Hey Nina, do you know anybody called Jane Sword?" asked Jack, "Yes! She's one of the servants! She's really the only person in the entire place that's actually nice to me! She kind of looks like you! In fact, what are your names?" asked Nina, "I'm Jack Sword, and this is Amy Arrow, Prince Lucas Shield the 1ˢᵗ, Mark Slingshot, and these pets are Fluffy, Sandie, and Meteor!" said Jack.

"Wait, Jack SWORD? You're related to Jane?!" said Nina, "Yes, she's my mom! That's why I asked! I really want to save her!" said Jack, "Well Then, I guess we could save her, also, Hello, your majesty Prince Lucas Shield!" said Nina, as she bowed to Lucas, "Oh, you don't have to do that! Anyway, what about saving Jack's mom?" asked Lucas, "Well, in order to get around the Team Rexfire Ninja Base, you need to be as agile and sneaky as a ninja! Let's see how agile and sneaky you guys are over in that field!" said Nina, "Ok, come on, let's go! Said Jack, "Yeah!" said Mark, and they went over to the field next to Combaido City.

"Ok, let's battle!" said Nina, when they arrived at the field, "What weapon are you using?" asked Jack, "A katana! It's kind of like a sword, but it's curved! It's mostly used by ninjas!" said Nina, "Ok!" said Jack, "But first, can you show me how you fight?" asked Nina, "Alright!" said Jack, and he showed her all of his sword fighting techniques! He showed her Dodge and Slash, Combo Slash, Mega Force, and Spinning Slash!

"Seriously? I bet I could beat you with my eyes closed!" laughed Nina, "Hey! That's a little rude, don't you think?" pestered Jack, "No, seriously! Put a blindfold on my eyes, I'll show you!" said Nina, and Amy took out a blindfold from her bag, and tied it around Nina's eyes! That meant that Nina couldn't see for the whole battle! "Ok, fine! Let's start!" said Jack, "3, 2, 1, Go!" shouted Lucas, and Jack charged at Nina! However, right when Jack was about to hit Nina's katana, Nina dodged the attack, without even seeing Jack! "Woah!" said Jack, and he charged at Nina again, and this time, Nina did a backflip to avoid Jack! She landed behind Jack, and pinned him to the floor, and knocked his sword out of his hand! She did all of this blindfolded! "Wow! How did you do that? Can you give me some tips?" asked Jack, "Sure! This is the first and most important thing to learn if you want to be a ninja, that is, that ninjas always do the unexpected! If a ninja is in a tricky situation, they can get out of it by doing what no-one expects!" said Nina, "Thanks Nina! Just one question, why were you running as fast as you could before?" asked Jack, "I don't have to tell you that if I don't want to!" replied Nina, sassily, "Anyway, isn't it time for us to save Jack's mother?" asked Lucas, "Oh yes, follow me, I'll lead you to the secret ninja base!" replied Nina, and they followed Nina back into the city, and walked past many cherry blossom trees, and walked under many glowing lanterns! They kept walking, and went a little bit out of the city, and then arrived at the ninja's base!

"We're here!" said Nina, "Uh, why is the building so small?" asked Mark, "Yeah, it looks like only a few ninjas could fit in there!" said Amy, "Most of the building is underground, that's why! Anyway, let's go inside!" said Nina, and they all walked inside, quietly.

Chapter 22

The Great Rescue

Jack, Amy, Fluffy, Lucas, Mark, and Nina had all just entered the secret ninja base in Combaido City! "Should we just leave Meteor and Sandie outside?" asked Amy, "Yeah, I think it'll be fine!" said Nina, and they snuck into the ninja's base, "Do you know where the servants stay?" asked Jack, Yes, I do! Once the sun sets, their work is done, and they have to stay in their rooms until the sunrise! Their rooms aren't very nice ones, of course, Team Rexfire would never use their money on that sort of thing!" whispered Nina, "I can't believe my mom has been here the whole time, and now I'm going to save her!" whispered Jack.

As they tiptoed through the base Nina saw some ninja costumes hanging on the wall, and told them all to put them on, so they did! They continued to walk, until they heard some ninjas talking! "The key – It's gone!" one of the ninjas said, "Oh no! Aria's coming tomorrow morning to collect it, it's already past midnight! She's going to be furious!" another ninja said, "We could even get thrown into the dungeons!" another ninja said, "Quick, tell all of the ninjas to search the hideout as thoroughly as possible!" the leader ninja shouted, furiously! For some reason, Nina was smiling at all this! "Why are you smiling?" asked Mark, "Oh, nothing!" replied Nina, "How can you possibly be smiling at a time like this! Now there's going to be ninjas all around the base!" whispered Jack, "Oh Jack, you don't think before you act, do you? The reason I told you to put on ninja costumes was so we would blend in with all the other ninjas, obviously!" said Nina, "Oh, yes." said Jack.

Soon enough, the entire hideout filled up with ninjas, and the group had to act like they were searching for the key! "Wait a minute, it all makes sense now! The key that the ninjas are looking for is the sixth key of The Seven Keys! That's why Aria is looking for it!" said Jack, "Yeah!" said Nina, "Look, There's your mom's room!" said Nina, "Yes!" said Jack, "Quick, open the door!" said Lucas, and Jack opened the door! Nina walked in first, "Hi Mrs. Sword, I have a surprise for you today, A very big one, in fact!" said Nina, "What could that be?" asked Mrs. Sword, "I present to you, your only son, Jack Sword!" said Nina, "W-Wait, Is this what I t-think it is?" said Mrs. Sword, and Jack walked into the room! "J-Jack, is that you?" asked Mrs. Sword, with tears in her eyes, "Yes mom! It's me!" replied Jack, joyfully, and he ran over and hugged her! Jack's mom was crying with joy! "After the happy reunion, Jack told his mom about all the adventures he'd been on, and how Mr. Sword was doing, Jack told her everything!

Jack's mom was so happy that she almost forgot that Nina was in the room! Once she remembered she said, "Thank you so, so much Nina, for bringing my son back to me!" said Mrs. Sword, "Yeah Nina, thank you so much!" thanked Jack, "Save the thanks for later, I have another surprise for you Jack!" said Nina.

Suddenly, Nina reached into her pocket, and took out a shiny golden key! "Wait, is that the sixth key of the Seven Keys?!" asked Jack, "Yes! This is the surprise! I was the one who stole the key! The sixth key of the Seven Keys, The Key of Niamh the Ninja!" said Nina, excitedly, "Seriously? Why is everything so ironic? Why does nobody seem to notice? The first key Aria dropped belonged to Julian the Warrior, who was friends with fairies, and it landed in Glimmer Woods, The Forest of Fairies! The second key belonged to Daria the Desert Merchant, and it landed in the desert! It's the same for all the other keys, including this one!" thought Mark.

"But why would you steal the sixth key? You're part of Team Rexfire!" asked Jack, "I already told you, I don't want to be part of Team Rexfire!" said Nina, as she handed Jack the key, suddenly, a ninja busted open the door! "Hey, that boy has the key!" he shouted, and a bunch of ninjas ran into the room! "Jack, Quick! Run away and get the key to safety! We'll protect your mom!" shouted Nina, so Jack started running, but it was too late!

Jack was surrounded by ninjas! "Oh no, what do I do, what do I do?" thought Jack. Suddenly, Jack had an idea! Nina's words echoed through Jack's head "Ninjas always do the unexpected!" when he remembered that, he thought as hard as he could, and then he got an incredible idea...

Chapter 23

The Great Escape

Jack, Amy, Lucas, Mark, Fluffy, and their new friend Nina had all just saved Jack's mom, with a little help from Nina! Nina had even given Jack the sixth key of the Seven Keys, and told him to bring it to safety! However, when Jack did that, he got into a bit of a tricky situation!

Jack was surrounded by Team Rexfire ninjas, but he had an idea on how to stop them! Nina's words echoed through Jack's head, "Ninjas always do the unexpected!" thought Jack, "That's it! I need to do the unexpected!" Jack thought, and then he closed his eyes, took a deep breath, and shouted, "Foggius Summonus!"

Suddenly, fog filled up the room! The ninjas couldn't see a thing! Jack ran out of the room, while the rest of the group fought the ninjas, and protected Jack's mom! "If Kyle the Wizard hadn't taught me that trick, I don't know what I would have done!" thought Jack, as he held onto the sixth key of the Seven Keys, tightly!

Meanwhile, Amy, Lucas, Mark, and Nina were protecting Jack's mom from the Team Rexfire Ninjas! Amy was using her bow and arrows, Lucas was using is sword and shield, Mark was using his slingshot, and Nina was using a katana, as well as a few ninja stars!

Jack kept running through the fog towards the door that led outside, but when he was about to get outside, there was somebody very surprising at the door! It was Aria! "Hey, what are you annoying key hunters doing here?!! Please don't tell me you stole the key I was supposed to collect, Argh!" shouted Aria, during all the chaos, "O-Oh no." quivered Jack, "Yeah, You should be scared. You are nothing compared to me! Wait, a second, is that my key you're holding?! Give it to me now, or else!" shouted Aria, "Or else what?" shouted Jack, having gotten his courage back. At this, Aria smirked and said, "I think it would be better that you don't know."

"Fine then, I challenge you to a sword duel!" shouted Jack, "Do you really think that's the best option, even after I crushed you back at the Diamond Dragon League?" said Aria, "Yes. Yes I do!" shouted Jack, and he charged at her and spun around, "Spinning Slash!" shouted Jack, "Seriously? Watch this!" shouted Aria, as she dodged Jack's Spinning Slash, "What?" said Jack, "Portal Attack!" shouted Aria, and she teleported behind him, and whacked his sword! Jack turned around, "Mega Force!" he shouted, knocking Aria back,

"You're better than you were before, but you're still no match for me!" shouted Aria, "I'm going to defeat you no matter what!" shouted Jack, "Too bad, Flaming Sword!" shouted Aria, and her sword went on fire! Just like before, Jack had no choice but to run away from a flaming sword! "Everybody run!" shouted Jack.

Amy, Fluffy, Lucas, Nina, Jack, and Jack's mom all ran out of the ninja base and jumped onto Meteor and Sandie, who were outside, and started riding away from the ninja base! The Team Rexfire Ninja's were still chasing them on horses, but eventually, they escaped from them! They continued riding, "Hey Jack, I'm pretty sure that you're going to say yes, but can I please join your team?" asked Nina, "Of course!" said Jack, "Thank you!" said Nina, "Thank you so much Jack, for saving me! I'm so excited to get back to Lighton Village and to see your father!" Jack's mom said, "That's exactly where we're heading mom!" said Jack, "You've still got the sixth key, right?" asked Lucas, "Yes!" said Jack, "So, does anyone know where we're going to look for the seventh and final key of the Seven Keys?" asked Mark, "What if we go to Snowfall Village?" asked Amy, "Sure!" said Jack, Anyway, Jack, can you please tell me about all the adventures you've been on?" Jack's mom asked, "Of course!" replied Jack, and they continued riding to Lighton Village for a few days, with Jack telling his mom about his adventures the whole time.

When they arrived in Lighton Village, Jack and his mom were very excited! "You guys wait on Meteor and Sandie, I can't wait to see how happy my dad will be! So Jack and his mom knocked on the door of their house! Soon enough, Jack's dad opened the door, and then when he saw them, he froze in shock! "Surprise!" said Jack, and then Jack's dad said warmly, "Thank you, my son Jack!"

Chapter 24

Snowfall Village

Jack and his friends had just dropped Jack's mom back home, and now Jack and his family were together again!

"Once again, Jack, thank you so much!" Jack's dad said, while hugging Jack's mom, "Yes Jack, thank you!" said Jack's mom, crying with joy, "Save the thank you for when I get the seventh key of the Seven Keys!" replied Jack, "Oh Jack, we're so proud of you!" Jack's dad said, "Thank you! Well I better get going to find that seventh key!" said Jack, "You're going so soon?" asked Jack's mom, "Come on mom, the whole country is at stake! I've got to find that final key! Bye!" said Jack, "Bye then, and god luck!" said Jack's dad, "Thank you, and bye!" said Jack, as he left.

"Hi everybody!" said Jack, "Did everything go well?" asked Amy, "Yes!" said Jack, "So, now we're heading to Snowfall Village next to Mount Alperia!" said Mark, "I heard there's an abandoned castle there!" said Lucas, "Cool! I guess we should get going!" said Nina, and they started riding on Meteor and Sandie.

"I still don't understand why it feels like Meteor is teleporting every once in a while! Look, Sandie and the others are way behind us!" said Jack, "I don't know, it's really weird! It looks like the speed potion that Kyle the Wizard gave us has worn off though!" replied Lucas.

They continued riding, "Why does Aria want to release Rexus anyway?" asked Jack, "I'm pretty sure she's training Rexus to listen to her commands!" said Lucas, "I know that, but why did she make Team Rexfire and for what does she want to use Rexus?" asked Jack, "My dad, King Leo, of course, told me all about it! Team Rexfire was formed way before Aria was born, it was first created by Aria's grandfather, Arthur! Their goal was to rule Julandia! If Arthur had succeeded in his plans to force my grandfather, King Liam, to give him the throne, Aria would have been queen, instead of me being the prince! Luckily, Arthur didn't succeed in his plans! So Arthur's son tried again, and didn't succeed, and now Aria is trying to take the throne!" said Lucas, "Interesting!" replied Jack.

Meanwhile, on Sandie, Mark was shivering, "It's so cold! How are none of you freezing right now?" he said, "Well, I think you're so cold because you're from the desert!" said Amy, "Yeah!" said Nina, "Look! We've arrived at the base of Mount Alperia!" said Lucas, "So, this is the highest mountain in Julandia!" said Mark, "Yes, this is the tallest in Julandia!"

replied Jack, "Look over there! It's Snowfall Village!" said Nina, and all of them started walking over to Snowfall Village!

It was snowing, and there were reindeer everywhere! "Aria's probably going to release Rexus very soon, so we should move a little bit faster!" suggested Lucas, "Alright! Everybody start running through the snow!" said Jack, "Ok!" all of them replied, and they started running!

Eventually, they arrived at Snowfall Village, and decided to find an inn to stay in for the night! When they found one, they went inside, and heard a man talking to another man, saying, "Mount Alperia may be the tallest mountain in Julandia, but it's not the tallest mountain in the world, it's only the third most tall! The two tallest mountains in the world are both in the kingdom of Skyvoria, where my family and I are from! The view on the top of Mount Cloudhigh, the tallest mountain in the world is beautiful!" the man said, "Wow!" the other man said, "Really? What is it like in Skyvoria?" asked Jack, "In Skyvoria, we have magical gliders that let you fly around!" the man replied, "Cool!" replied Jack, "I'm staying here so I can visit Alperia Castle, on top of Mount Alperia!" the other man said, "Wait, that's a place?" asked Jack, "Yes, of course it is! It's a historic place! Sadly, the castle was partly destroyed 300 years ago, by Rexus when he first came to Julandia! However, the ruins of the castle still stand!" the man replied, "Wow!" said Jack.

"I think I know where we're going to look for the seventh key!" said Jack, when he went back to the others, "Really?

Where?" asked Nina, "We're going to Alperia Castle!" replied Jack, "Isn't that place supposed to be in ruins?" asked Mark, "Only partly!" said Jack, "Then it's settled, we're going to Alperia Castle tomorrow!" announced Lucas, and they stayed in the inn for the night.

Chapter 25

Mount Alperia

Jack, Amy, Lucas, Mark, Nina, Fluffy, Sandie, and Meteor had all just woken up in Snowfall Village, and they were ready to climb Mount Alperia to reach Alperia Castle!

They all ran out of the inn, and ran through the snowy plains, and arrived at the base of Mount Alperia! "Wow, it's so tall!" said Jack, "Yeah, obviously, it's the tallest mountain Julandia!" replied Mark, "How are we supposed to climb it?" asked Nina, "Oh, I didn't think about that!" said Jack, "See Jack, you never think things through!" said Nina, "I could help you!" somebody said, "Who are you?" asked Lucas, "I'm Stephen! The man you met at the inn in Snowfall Village, remember?" the man said, "Oh yes! I'm Jack, and these are Amy, Lucas, Mark, Nina, and Fluffy! How can you help Stephen?" asked Jack.

"I have a few skysuits!" replied Stephen, "What's a skysuit?" asked Nina, "A skysuit is a thing used in Skyvoria to catch air and glide around! Skysuits are really popular in Skyvoria! They're not used very much in Julandia and another kingdom called Oceanovia, but they're very common in Skyvoria!" replied Stephen, "Wow! So that means we can put on the skysuits, and because it's so windy here, we'll go flying up!" said Jack, "Exactly!" said Stephen.

Stephen handed the skysuits to Jack, Amy, Lucas, Mark, and Nina, and then put on his own one, while they put on theirs!

"Now, before we fly, you need to learn the basics of using a skysuit... Hey Jack, where are you going?" asked Stephen, "Why do we need to learn the basics? This should be so easy, watch this!" said Jack, and he ran over to the mountain and jumped as high as he could! Suddenly, Jack caught the wind and went flying into the sky, "Wow! Woohoo!" shouted Jack, as he went flying up into the air!

"Jack, are you sure you know how to control yourself when you're in the air?" asked Stephen, "How hard could it be?" replied Jack, but then suddenly he went flying into the mountain, but luckily turned around just in time, Jack couldn't control himself in the air! Jack started falling down, but then, luckily, Stephen jumped up, started flying, and caught Jack in mid-air! "Phew!" said Jack, "Thank goodness!" said Stephen, as he brought Jack down to safety.

"Sorry about that!" said Jack, "No problem!" replied Stephen. "So, I guess it's time for us to learn how to use a skysuit!" said Lucas, "Yes!" replied Stephen, and so, they learned how to control themselves in the air while using a skysuit!

When they finished learning, they were ready to fly up to the top of Mount Alperia, and that's what they did! It was quite challenging, but they flew up to the top of Mount Alperia!

"Wow that was fun!" said Mark, when they reached the top of Mount Alperia, "Look, there's Alperia Castle!" said Amy, "Yes! Anyway, why are you guys even trying to reach Alperia Castle?" asked Stephen, "We're looking for the Seven Keys, for King Leo!" said Jack, "What are the Seven Keys? I don't know, I'm from Skyvoria, remember?" asked Stephen, so they all told Stephen the story of the Seven Keys!

"Wow! That's crazy!" said Stephen, after hearing the story of the Seven Keys, "yeah, I know!" said Jack, "But anyway, I need to go now, so, bye!" said Stephen, "Ok, bye! It was nice meeting you!" said Jack, "Bye!" everybody else said.

"Now, I guess it's time to check out Alperia Castle!" said Jack, "More like Alperia Ruins!" said Lucas, "Yeah, look at it! It's partly destroyed!" said Amy, "Yeah!" said Nina, "Yeah, I know, but the seventh key of the Seven Keys could still have fallen there!" said Jack, "Ok!" said Mark, and they all walked to the castle!

"I wonder if the seventh key is here..." said Jack, "Yeah!" said Nina, "Look up there! I think I see the seventh key, but it's all the way up at the top of the castle! I can see it because the ceiling's broken! But there's a problem!" said Mark, "What's the problem?" asked Lucas, "The stairs that lead to the top floor of the castle are broken!" "Oh no! What do we do?" asked Jack, "Too bad I don't have my rope!" said Amy, "Don't worry! I already know what to do! Just leave it all up to me!" replied Nina.

Chapter 26

The Final Key

Jack and his friends had just arrived inside of Alperia Castle on Mount Alperia, and Mark had spotted the seventh and final key of the Seven Keys on the top floor of Alperia Castle, needed to lock the cage on top of Irupt Volcano, to lock up Rexus again, and stop Team Rexfire!

"How can you reach the top floor of Alperia Castle?" asked Jack, "I'm a ninja, and one of the advanced moves you learn when you're a ninja, is running up and on walls!" replied Nina, "Oh, I get it! You're going to run up the stone walls of the castle to get the seventh key!" said Lucas, "Exactly, because the stone wall isn't smooth, I can run up it easily!" said Nina, and she hopped onto the wall and started running up it!

"Wow! That's impressive!" said Jack, "Definitely!" said Lucas, and Nina kept running up to the top of the castle!

When she reached the top, she saw the seventh key! "Guys, I've reached the top, but there's another problem!" said Nina, "What's the problem?" asked Jack, "There's a sleeping Snowfroster up here! If I try to grab the key, it might wake up!" said Nina, "A Snowfroster?! Those things are really aggressive ice beasts!" said Lucas, "Luckily, it looks like there's also a rope up here! You guys can use it to climb up here!" said Nina, and she dropped down the rope to Jack and the others! They caught the rope, and while Nina was holding the rope they climbed up to the top of the castle!

"Wow! It really is a Snowfroster! I've never seen one of them before!" said Jack, "Well, luckily it's sleeping, but if I try to grab the key, it's going to wake up!" said Nina, "Let's just slowly tiptoe over!" whispered Jack, and he slowly tiptoed over to the Snowfroster!

As he tiptoed, the Snowfroster twitched its ear! Jack gasped quickly! Luckily, the Snowfroster didn't wake up! Jack took the key as gently as he could, but then he made the huge mistake of screaming, "Yes!" after he got the seventh key! Hearing this, the Snowfroster woke up!

"Oh no!" shouted Jack, as he held the seventh key, and the Snowfroster growled!

"Seriously Jack! We almost had the seventh and final key, but then you screamed yes and woke up the Snowfroster! Now how are we going to get of this mess!" shouted Nina, "Sorry!" said Jack, and the Snowfroster got up and started chasing everyone! Jack took out his sword, "Spinning Slash!" shouted

Jack, and he attacked the Snowfroster, but then the Snowfroster breathed ice out of its mouth! "The ice breath from a Snowfroster can freeze you solid Jack, be careful!" said Lucas, and ran into the battle with his sword out and ready!

Lucas attacked the Snowfroster with his sword, but the Snowfroster continued attacking! Jack dodged all of its ice breaths, and struck back with a powerful Combo Slash! So far, they were doing great! Amy started blasting arrows at the Snowfroster, but they were all frozen in an instant! This was the point that the battle got a lot harder!

The Snowfroster roared for help, and then two other Snowfrosters came! "Oh no! Now it's going to be three times harder to defeat them!" said Jack, Mark and Nina also started helping, but then one of the Snowfrosters froze Fluffy solid! "Oh no! What do I do?" cried Amy, "Just shoot the ice with an arrow! It's actually quite thin, so don't shoot it too hard!" replied Lucas, "Ok!" said Amy, and she shot the ice cube that Fluffy was in with an arrow! The ice broke and Fluffy was freed!

They continued fighting the Snowfrosters, until Nina scared off one of them, and Lucas scared off another one! There was only one Snowfroster left, the first one, and it was the most powerful one! Jack continued fighting it, until he pulled off the most powerful move he had done yet! "Winning Strike!" Jack shouted, as he jumped in the air and slashed down at the Snowfroster!

The Snowfroster roared with pain and ran away, leaving Jack and his friends with the seventh and final key! "Now I can scream yes!" said Jack, "Yeah, you can!" said Mark, "Yes! We finally have all of the Seven Keys!" screamed Jack, "Yes, and now we have the seventh key, the key of Buster the Blacksmith!" said Lucas! "Now that we have all of the Seven Keys, it's time to head to Irupt Volcano to lock the cage on it!" said Amy, happily, "Yeah!" said Jack, joyfully.

Chapter 27

The Battle Begins

Jack and his friends had just found the seventh and final key of the Seven Keys, which they needed to lock the cage on top of Irupt Volcano, to teleport Rexus into the cage, to stop Aria and Team Rexfire, and save Julandia!

They ran out of Alperia Castle, and happily, jumped onto Meteor and Sandie, and rode into Snowfall Village! However, when they arrived at Snowfall Village, they found out about a shocking surprise!

When they arrived at Snowfall Village, they saw some of the king's messengers riding through the town and shouting, "Aria has released Rexus! Rexus is attacking the capital city of New Deyal! The king's soldiers need all the help they can get! Please go to New Deyal, they need as much help as they can get!" the messengers shouted, and they kept repeating this same speech! The citizens on Snowfall Village were panicking, in fact, everyone in Julandia was panicking, including Jack and his friends! "We're too late!" said Mark, "We're not too late yet, we can still save Julandia!" shouted Jack.

"Yeah! We still can! We just need to get to Irupt Volcano as fast as we can!" said Lucas, "But there's a problem, the quickest way to Irupt Volcano is through New Deyal!" said Mark, "Well, we're just going to have to find a way through there!" said Lucas.

Meteor seemed to understand everything Lucas was saying for some reason, and suddenly, her eyes started glowing a brilliant blue! "What's happening to you Meteor?!" asked Lucas, when suddenly, Meteor started floating in the air! Then, lots of magical energy seemed to spin around Meteor! Suddenly, there was a horn growing from Meteor's head, and wings appeared on Meteor's back! Meteor wasn't a horse anymore, she was a magical unicorn with wings! "Wow! Meteor's turned into a unicorn with wings! That explains all the magical teleporting Meteor was doing! She was a unicorn the whole time!" said Lucas, joyfully!

"Meteor was a unicorn the whole time?!" asked Jack, "I've heard about this before! Unicorns often disguise themselves as horses in front of humans!" said Mark.

"Oh yes! I've also heard that they only transform into beautiful unicorns during emergencies!" said Amy, "This is awesome! Now we can fly straight over New Deyal to get to Irupt Volcano!

"But all of us can't fit on Meteor, and I doubt Sandie can move as fast as a unicorn, so what do I do?" asked Mark, "Well, when we got the fifth key, Kyle the Wizard gave me an extra speed potion, so you could just give it to Sandie!" suggested Lucas, "Ok!" replied Mark, "Anyway, let's get flying!" said Jack.

They jumped onto Meteor as a unicorn, and Meteor jumped into the sky and started flapping her wings majestically! Meteor flew through the air very fast, while Sandie was following her with a speed potion! Jack, Amy, Fluffy and Lucas were on Meteor, while Mark and Nina were on Sandie!

They flew over all of the cities they had been to, Lighton Village, Plankteff Town, Rodeo Town, and many of the other towns, villages, and cities that they visited! "We've visited lots of places, and made lots of friends on this adventure! It really was a great journey, and now it's almost over!" said Jack, "Remember Jack, Meteor, Nina, and I will hold back the dragon in New Deyal, while Amy and Mark hold back the Team Rexfire members! It's all up to you to stop Aria, and then climb up Irupt Volcano, and lock the cage with The Seven Keys!" said Lucas, as he handed Jack the Seven Keys. Jack looked at the keys, they reminded him about all the adventures they had been on! They had been through jungles and deserts, mountains and beaches, forests and cities, and they had even been to a magical village!

Now it was time for all of them to stop Rexus and Team Rexfire, and save all of Julandia! "I'm going to win against Aria this time. Definitely!" thought Jack, as they flew on Meteor! Jack took out his sword he had gotten at the Diamond Dragon League, "This sword was the second place prize for the Diamond Dragon League! It's very powerful, and it's because I lost to Aria that I got this sword! If I had won in the Diamond Dragon League, I would've just gotten 50 gold coins! So sometimes it might help you out in the future, if you lose in the present! Anyway, it's time to defeat Aria, Rexus, and Team Rexfire once and for all!" thought Jack.

Chapter 28

The Battle Continues

Jack and his friends had just found out that Aria had fully trained Rexus, and how Aria, Rexus, and the rest of Team Rexfire were attacking the capital city of Julandia, New Deyal! Jack and his friends needed to get to New Deyal as fast as they could, but they didn't know how, until they discovered that Meteor was actually a unicorn with wings in disguise the whole time! So Jack, Amy, Fluffy and Lucas were on Meteor, while Mark and Nina were on Sandie!

Jack and his friends eventually reached New Deyal, and they flew over New Deyal to the base of Irupt Volcano, nearby to New Deyal! They landed there, and saw all the chaos that was happening in New Deyal! "Oh no! What do we do?" asked Nina, "How about Mark and Amy help to hold back the Team Rexfire Members, while Lucas and Nina fight off Rexus, while I battle Aria!" suggested Jack, "Great Idea!" said Lucas and they prepared for the greatest battle that they had ever had!

Rexus was burning all of New Deyal, and King Leo's soldiers were holding it back!

Lucas and Nina ran over to Rexus, and Lucas almost hit by Rexus's fire breath! King Leo was commanding the soldiers, and Lucas ran up to him! "Dad, what do I do?" asked Lucas, "Lucas, you're here! We've found out that Rexus's weak point is the gem on his chest, so were attacking that part of him! He's huge though, so it's not making much of a difference!" said King Leo, "Well I guess Nina and I will attack Rexus's gem on his chest then! I just hope that Jack can lock the cage on top of Irupt Volcano before Rexus's burns down New Deyal, and eventually all of New Deyal!" said Lucas, and Lucas and Nina started fighting Rexus!

Meanwhile Aria was smiling at all of this on top of Irupt Volcano!

Meanwhile, Mark and Amy were helping some of the king's soldiers to fight off all the Team Rexfire members!

Jack was standing at the bottom of Irupt Volcano, when suddenly he saw Kyle the Wizard run up to him! "Jack! I see you're trying to get the Seven Keys into the cage on top of the volcano!" said Kyle, "Yes!" said Jack, "Well Aria's standing up there! You're going to need to battle her if you want to get to Rexus's cage! I know! Take this strength potion, and this lava resistance potion! They'll help you out when you're battling Aria!" said Kyle, "Thanks!" said Jack and he drank the two potions and said goodbye to Kyle!

Jack started climbing up Irupt Volcano, and that was no easy task! There were huge boulders falling down from the top of the volcano, and Jack had to dodge them! Jack continued climbing, and he started feeling very hot! When Jack reached the top of Irupt Volcano, he was covered in sweat! Suddenly, he saw Aria, standing at the top of Irupt Volcano, menacingly!

"This is going to be the hardest battle ever!" thought Jack, "Well, well, well, looks like Jack Sword is here to save Julandia! Well too bad, you're too late! Hand over the Seven Keys!" said Aria, "I'll never hand over the Seven Keys!" shouted Jack, and he drew his sword from its sheath, "Oh really, you think you can win against me in a sword-fighting battle, even though you've already lost to me twice!" laughed Aria, "Yes, I do think – no, I believe that I can win against you in a sword fighting battle!" declared Jack, and Jack charged at Aria with immense force, but Aria blocked it with her sword, and immediately attacked back with a fierce swing of her sword! Jack dodged it and used Spinning Slash against Aria, but then Aria dodged that and attacked using a Portal Attack, where she teleported behind Jack and struck his sword!

Jack used a Combo Slash, and then, suddenly Aria took out another sword and started using dual swords! "Hey, that's cheating!" shouted Jack, "It's not like this is some official Sword-Fighting League match or anything, nothing is cheating!" replied Aria, and she used a new move called Dual Strike, where she jumped into the air and slashed down at Jack's sword with her two swords! Suddenly, when Aria slashed down at Jack's swords, he saw Aria's sword made a cut in his arm straight down the middle! Jack clutched his arm in pain, and now he knew he was at a huge disadvantage, but he also knew that he had to win this, to save Julandia!

He had to win this battle, no matter what!

Chapter 29

Let's Save Julandia!

Jack and his friends were right in the middle of the most intense battle they had ever fought! Lucas, Nina, and some of Jack's other friends, like Stephen, Bella, and Richard were battling Rexus with King Leo and his soldiers, while Mark, Amy, Amy's dad and his crew, and Kyle the Wizard were battling Team Rexfire members, and of course, Jack was battling Aria, the leader of Team Rexfire!

"Thank goodness Kyle the Wizard gave me that strength potion, otherwise this cut would have hurt a lot more!" thought Jack, as he caught his breath until, suddenly, Aria laughed, as she looked at her sword! Jack knew what she was going to do next, she was going to light her sword on fire!

Jack remembered that he had lost to Aria twice before because of her Flaming Sword, but he knew he wasn't going to lose this time, no matter what! This time Jack faced Aria bravely! He wasn't scared of Aria's flaming sword because Kyle the Wizard had given him a fire resistance potion! Aria lit her sword on fire, except, her sword got bigger, and the fire – it was blue! "Oh no, I should have expected Aria to have a surprise planned for this battle!" thought Jack, "Aren't you going to run away this time Jack? Or are you just frozen in fear!" shouted Aria, but Jack wasn't going to do either of those things, he was going to think things through, as Nina had advised him to do, many times.

Suddenly, Jack had an idea! It sparked in his mind like a bolt of lightning! He had a .little bit of his fire resistance potion left, and he splashed it onto his sword! He was ready, to face Aria!

Jack charged at Aria, braver than he'd ever been! As he charged, he thought about his mom, and his dad, and all the friends he'd made all across Julandia, and how they were all counting on him! Aria wasn't expecting this, and she tried to block the attack with her sword, but then, suddenly, Jack had sparks in his eyes, he seemed so much braver and stronger this time! "Ultimate Super Slash!" shouted Jack, and his sword started almost glowing! Jack threw back his sword, and then slashed his sword forward with all his might, and Aria couldn't stop that! Aria tried to hold Jack's sword back as hard as she could, but then she noticed her sword begin to crack! The crack was getting bigger! "There's no way you can defeat me this time!" shouted Jack, as Aria's sword broke in two! Jack struck Aria with the most powerful blow he'd ever done! **BOOM!**

Aria's sword shattered into pieces, and Aria fell of the volcano, and disappeared, shouting, "My boss is going to be so disappointed in me!"

"I wonder who Aria's boss is!" thought Jack, and then Jack realised that victory was right in front of him! All he needed to do was climb a little bit further up, to reach the cage that Rexus was going to be trapped in!

Jack climbed up to the cage joyfully, thinking about how proud of him everyone was going to be! Jack also felt a little bit nervous, but he faced his fears and climbed up bravely!

Jack had almost reached the top, when suddenly, he heard some sort of loud rumbling coming from the volcano! In fact, everyone heard the loud rumbling coming from the volcano! Everyone looked up at Jack, who realised what was happening...

Irupt Volcano was erupting! "This is the worst timing ever!" thought Jack, as the volcano continued rumbling, everybody saw a huge spew of lava and smoke come out of the volcano!

Jack rushed to the cage and took out the Seven Keys, and remembered where each one was from! The key of Julian the Warrior, which they found in the Fairy Village, The key of Daria the Merchant, Cactarab Town, The key of George the Explorer, found in Maja Jungle, The key of Sammy the Pirate, found at New Sealand, The key of Oscar the Craftsman, found at Mystical Village, The key of Niamh the Ninja, found at Combaido City, and the key of Buster the Blacksmith, found in Alperia Castle! Jack took out each key and locked each lock with them, all seven of them! What happened next, made Jack Sword a great hero!

Chapter 30

The Legend of Jack

Jack Sword had just locked the seven locks that were in the cage that was on Irupt Volcano with the Seven Keys!

When Jack locked the final lock with the final key, a huge beam of light, so bright that you couldn't even look at his, blasted out of Irupt Volcano, and the volcano stopped erupting! The powerful beam of light went flying towards Rexus, and Rexus roared in fear, because he knew what was coming next! The powerful beam of light hit Rexus, and created a huge explosion of light! When the explosion was over everyone saw that Rexus had disappeared, and when Jack looked into the cage beside him, Rexus was there! Rexus looked a lot weaker, and he fell in defeat!

"WOOHOO!" shouted Jack as he jumped with joy, and he ran down the volcano joyfully! Everybody cheered, except for the other Team Rexfire members, who ran away, angrily, while the crowd shouted "Jack Sword! Jack Sword! Jack Sword! Jack Sword! Jack Sword! Hooray for the Legendary Jack Sword!"

Jack was so happy, and the first thing he did when he came down to the bottom of the volcano, was hug all of his friends, and shout, "Don't just thank me, thank all my friends as well, there are so many people that helped me get the Seven Keys and defeat Rexus, so you should thank them too!"

Then, King Leo shouted out loud, "Everybody come to the castle in New Deyal, I have a very special announcement to make! So everybody went to the castle in New Deyal, and took their seats!

King Leo began his announcement, "Greetings, Everyone, I am very happy to announce that Jack Sword, Amy Arrow, Prince Lucas Shield, Mark Slingshot, and Nina Katana have officially found The Seven Keys, and defeated Rexus and returned him to his cage on top of Irupt Volcano, which means they have officially saved Julandia!" King Leo said, joyfully, and everybody cheered and clapped their hands!

"As a reward for this great feat, Jack Sword and Mark Slingshot will be becoming knights, once they're old enough, and when they complete their training! King Leo announced, "What about me, dad?" asked Lucas, "You're already a prince, Lucas, that's a higher rank than a knight!" replied King Leo, "Anyway, in honour of Jack Sword and his friends, the statue of a knight in Alperia Castle will be replaced by a statue of Jack Sword and his friends! Also, Alperia Castle will be rebuilt and renovated! That's all for my speech, I hope everybody liked it!" said King Leo, and there was a huge applause, and everybody was congratulating Jack and his friends on the way out of the castle!

The next thing Jack did was travel back home on Meteor, who was a regular horse again, with his friends! When Jack arrived at his home in Lighton Village, he knocked on the door happily, and Mr. Sword and Mrs. Sword opened the door and immediately hugged Jack!

"Thank you so much, son, for everything you've done!" said Mr. Sword, as he hugged Jack, "How about we have a sword battle, just like when you first started your journey!" Jack's dad suggested, "Of course dad!" said Jack, and they both got their swords out, and got ready for battle, both of them smiling at each other! "3, 2, 1, Go!" shouted Mark, and Jack charged at Mr. Sword, and did a perfect Combo Slash! Jack's dad fumbled around with the sword, but he luckily caught it!

"Wow Jack, you really are better than you were at the start of your journey!" Jack's dad laughed, "Thanks a lot!" said Jack, and then Jack's dad charged at him and tried to hit his sword, but Jack perfectly dodged it and struck back with a strong blow!

Jack attacked again and again, until Mr. Sword's sword was knocked out of his hand!

"Looks like you won Jack! Again, thank you so much for everything you've done!" said Mr. Sword,

"No problem!" said Jack, smiling with joy.

Jack and his friends had been through forests and fields, deserts and mountains, cities and villages, they had even been to the creepy jungle, and they had even sailed the deep blue sea! They had defeated scary villains, and reunited happy families, they had even saved Julandia! By doing all these things, they became heroes!

THE END!

"We'd love if you could review our book!"

Please send your feedback / queries to

authordion@gmail.com

Other books from the author

Dion George

Ten Amazing Animal Stories

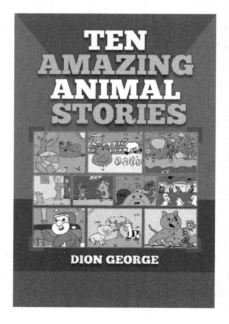

Read on Amazon Kindle Books

CPSIA information can be obtained
at www.ICGtesting.com
Printed in the USA
BVHW080810040122
625374BV00002B/85

9 781739 764302